Wild Moonlight

MIRIAM MINGER

This book is a work of fiction. Any reference to historical events, real people, or real locales are used fictitiously. Other names, characters, places, and incidents are the product of the author's imagination, and any resemblance to actual events or locales or persons, living or dead, is entirely coincidental.

Publishing History

Digital edition published by Walker Publishing
Copyright © 2016 by Miriam Minger

Print edition published by Walker Publishing
Copyright © 2016 by Miriam Minger

ISBN: 978-1-943644-13-1

Wild Moonlight

Book 3 of The O'Byrne Brides Series

Her thrilling tales of intense emotion, edge-of-your-seat adventure, and breathtaking sensuality have fired the imagination of readers everywhere. Here's what the critics are saying about award-winning author Miriam Minger...

"Outstanding! This is a well-written, moving story that shows the tremendous skill of the author. *Marvelous* barely describes my feelings."
— *Rendezvous*

"Five stars...should be at the top of your shopping list! Miriam Minger is a fifty-carat jewel!"
— *Affaire de Coeur*

"With Miriam Minger, you're assured of a good read!"
— *Heartland Critiques*

"Miriam Minger is a master storyteller who illustrates the full gamut of emotions felt by her characters. Emotions so strong that you are pulled into the pages and into their lives."
— *Inside Romance*

Other Books By Miriam Minger

The O'Byrne Brides Series
Wild Angel
Wild Roses
Wild Moonlight
On A Wild Winter's Night

The Man Of My Dreams Series
Secrets of Midnight
My Runaway Heart
My Forbidden Duchess

Captive Brides Collection
Twin Passions
Captive Rose
The Pagan's Prize

Dangerous Masquerade Collection
The Brigand Bride
The Temptress Bride
The Impostor Bride

To Love A Billionaire Series
The Maiden and the Billionaire
The Governess and the Billionaire
The Pirate Queen and the Billionaire
The Highland Bride and the Billionaire

Contemporary Romantic Suspense
Operation Hero

PROLOGUE

Ostmentown, Ireland, 1212
North of Dublin along the River Liffey

"Plague us no more with your tears, Nora MacTorkil! You shame us all if you continue to carry on so! Your father has decreed that you shall wed, and so you shall. If your sister had lived, God rest her, she would have wed on the morrow, but she did not and so the duty to our family rests with you!"

Our family? Nora rested her forehead upon the shuttered window and closed her eyes against the hot tears blinding her.

In vain she tried to close her mind against her stepmother Agnes's shrill words that still rang in her ears.

The woman wasn't her true family at all, but a second wife who had married Nora's father Magnus last summer only days after her beloved mother had fallen ill and died.

A sharp-tongued shrew of a woman who had swayed Magnus with an ambitious plan to marry off Nora's twin sister until poor Kristina had taken to her sickbed as well.

A sickbed that soon became a deathbed, Kristina laid to rest beside their mother while the cruel weight of Agnes's plans fell upon Nora. Swept by nausea at the thought of the man she would wed, Nora bit her lip hard to keep from retching.

"Such a fortunate bride you will be!" enthused Agnes, who paced with agitation behind her. "My cousin Sigurd Knutson is cousin as well to Earl Hakon of Norway and one of his most famed warriors—and Earl Hakon will be *king* one day. Think of it! The MacTorkils of Ostmentown will be joined by marriage to the royal house of Norway. With such an alliance it will not be long before the Ostmen of Éire gain strength enough again to challenge these accursed Normans!"

Sigurd Knutson. Now Nora could not prevent the bitter bile from filling her mouth.

Not a man, but a monster, her husband-to-be. She was just turned eighteen while he was fourteen years her senior, and already with four wives rotting in their graves.

None had borne him a legitimate heir and so Nora was to be his fifth bride, his animal lusts rumored to be as voracious as his thirst for an enemy's blood upon his sword. He stood nearly seven feet tall and had earned the name Skullcrusher in battle for his love of shattering men's skulls with his bare hands—

"To bed with you now, Nora, and no more tears! Do you hear me? It's bad enough your sister was the beauty while you're only passing fair. Your face is red and swollen as it is without more of this useless weeping!"

A sharp clap of Agnes's hands brought two maidservants running, and Nora found herself propelled by them toward the bed. Agnes, thin as a pole, her lovely features marred by a perpetual frown, followed close behind.

Nora did not fight the busy hands removing her lustrous blue silk gown for an equally fine sleeping gown, only the most exquisite fabrics adorning the daughter of the richest merchant in Dublin. As much Irish blood as Viking blood ran through the MacTorkil line after centuries of intermingling, but her father believed himself Norse first and so he had agreed all too readily with Agnes's plan.

The Norse in Éire who had long since called themselves Ostmen hated the Normans, and Magnus was no different even though he traded with them. It was his distant cousin after all, Asculf MacTorkil, the King of Dublin, who had been cast out by the ruthless invaders forty years past, the Ostmen forced to settle outside the city walls north of the River Liffey. Why not give consent to a marriage that might bring them closer to vengeance?

A marriage Nora was certain would lead her to an early grave like all of Sigurd Skullcrusher's other wives—God help her!

"Enough!" Agnes snapped at the maidservants as they helped Nora, trembling now, into bed. "At first light the women will return to help you bathe and wash your hair, unruly mess as it is. Pity it's not silken blond as was your sister's. How is it that two could share a womb and look so different? One so beautiful and the other almost plain—aye, thank God you've your father's wealth to secure you a fine husband! You'd not win one without it."

Fine husband? Nora clutched the covers under her chin as Agnes turned on her heel and went to the door, the two maidservants extinguishing all but one candle and scurrying out of the room ahead of her.

An instant later Nora was alone, her eyes welling again even though Agnes had thrown a last disapproving glance over her shoulder before closing the door.

Yet there was nothing Nora could do. She could no more stop the tears streaming down her face than she could quell the panic rising in her breast.

Tomorrow night she would be a bride.

Sharing a bed with her brute of a husband as he...as he...

No, she couldn't think of it!

Nor would she think of how Sigurd Skullcrusher had leered at her in the feasting-hall tonight, his head shaved and emblazoned with tattoos, his broad face scarred by the pox, his callused hands massive around his ale cup and his fingers thick, his battle-honed body so broad at the chest and shoulders that he looked a giant even seated at the table.

A giant that tomorrow night would pin her down and spread her legs while he covered her mouth with a massive palm to still her screams—

"No! Jesu, help me, no!" Despair overwhelming her, Nora threw back the covers and sprang from the bed. She spun for a moment in her bare feet, looking with desperation at the door to her bedchamber and then to the nearest shuttered window.

She could not stay here awaiting her fate like a lamb to the slaughter. She must run! Flee!

Her heart pounding fiercely, she took only an instant to don a pair of leather slippers and then she darted to the window. There she unlatched the shutters and threw them open to a balmy summer breeze wafting into the room. At once the single lit candle near the door was snuffed out, leaving Nora in darkness but for the ghostly light spilling across the floor from the ripe full moon.

With a start she realized she looked like a ghost, too, in her stark white sleeping gown that would alert anyone to her flight.

Growing frantic that Agnes or one of the maidservants might return to check on her, Nora ran to an ornate clothing chest and flung open the lid. Wildly she dug through silken gowns to find a dark cloak with a hood, which she pulled out and whirled around herself. She dug again to find a soft leather pouch that held jeweled brooches and arm-rings given to her by her parents. Her fingers trembled as she secured the pouch's golden cord around her wrist, and then she fled back to the window.

As she hoisted herself onto the narrow ledge, she could hear carousing and raucous laughter coming from the distant feasting-hall, and that only increased her panic. She was so desperate to flee that she threw herself out of the window to land hard on her side upon the ground, knocking the breath from her body. Yet she didn't hesitate, gasping as she drew the hood over her thick auburn hair and rose shakily to her feet.

Rows of longhouses made up her father's stronghold rimming the River Liffey, her next obstacle the guarded palisade. Fresh despair seized her as she kept her head down and ran quickly from the shadow of one building to the next toward the main gate.

How would she ever make her way out? Her only comfort lay in that most everyone was still celebrating in the feasting-hall, her furtive flight garnishing little notice. She could have cried aloud with relief when she spied a wagon drawn by two lumbering draft horses making its way toward the main gate. She ran hard to catch up, her lungs burning. With a desperate lunge she pulled herself aboard and squeezed between empty ale barrels to hide herself in the nick of time.

"Not a drop left for us, man?" a guard called out to the driver as the tall heavy gates creaked open.

"I'm bound to the storehouse for more barrels!" the driver said with an incredulous laugh. "These Norsemen are sure to drink Lord MacTorkil dry this night!"

"No surprise with eight shiploads of them come from Norway for the wedding. And from the size of the groom, I'd wager he drinks enough for five men."

"Aye, he finished off a barrel all on his own! Split it open with his axe and drank it down in one swallow!"

Sickened by their approving laughter, Nora ducked her head and prayed with all her might that she not be discovered.

Prayed that clouds would hide the bright full moon that shone so mercilessly down upon her. Only when she heard the heavy gates thudding shut behind the wagon did she dare to take a deep breath.

The driver was headed to one of her father's storehouses alongside the river.

The river where ships bound for distant places lined the docks.

All she had to do was board one of those ships and hide herself just as she'd done in the wagon.

Hide herself and hope the ship, once it set sail, would take her far away from Sigurd Skullcrusher and the cruel fate he had in store for her.

CHAPTER 1

Glenmalure
Wicklow Mountains, Leinster

"No, Ronan, Niall is *not* dead. He can't be dead! How can you say such a terrible thing about your brother?"

Horrified by the words that her husband had just uttered, Triona stared up at him in dismay as they lay together in bed. She'd seen Ronan Black O'Byrne, the feared rebel chieftain of the Glenmalure O'Byrnes, angry many times before but never with such a dark countenance upon him.

No, not even when his beloved sister Maire had ridden away three days past with Lord Duncan FitzWilliam to become his bride.

The Baron of Longford in Meath, no less, one of the most powerful Norman lords in Éire.

Truly, Triona had feared Ronan might kill the man when the two had clashed with swords outside the O'Byrne stronghold, Lord Duncan come by himself to Glenmalure to claim Maire for his own. Triona had run in anguish toward Ronan to try to stop their fighting, but it had taken gentle sweet Maire to stand up to her eldest brother and proclaim her love for Duncan and that she wished to be his wife.

Oh, aye, Ronan's face had been thunderous that day, too, when he had said Maire would be dead to them if she left with Duncan, and then he'd turned his back to her. Yet thank God he had somehow found forgiveness in his heart to turn around to watch Maire and Duncan ride from Glenmalure...and granted them the only blessing he could.

Triona had stood within Ronan's embrace that day, their little daughter Deirdre cradled in her arms as she, too, watched Maire leave her home and family behind for the man she loved. Just as Triona lay nestled in Ronan's arms right now, his magnificent body so wondrously warm and yet with tension emanating from every muscle.

He loved his brother Niall, she had no doubt of it, and had feared for him since he'd disappeared two months ago. Yet for Ronan to say now that Niall might be dead—

"Aye, Triona, it's true, he cannot be dead. If he was I would feel it. *Know* it."

Triona nodded and snuggled closer to Ronan, relieved to hear that he had relented from his harsh stance as she rested her hand upon his chest. His heartbeat thrilled her, so steady and strong, like the man she loved more than life itself.

"We would both know it, husband. One day Niall will

return home, aye, a changed man, to be sure. How could he not be after waiting for two years to marry Caitlin MacMurrough only to have her choose another man over him? He truly loved her and believed she loved him, too. Begorra, it was an awful thing to have to share such news with him. To see the light die in his eyes—"

"It's for the best, harsh as it sounds. We've a fragile peace between the O'Byrnes and the MacMurroughs. If Caitlin's heart wasn't fully in the match, then she spared Niall from an unhappy marriage and us, from an unhappy Donal MacMurrough. Your uncle holds a great fondness for you, but we need no such strife that might turn our clans once more into enemies."

Triona fell silent, praying that such a day might never come. It was a wondrous thing to know some measure of peace, Ronan even suspending his raids against the Normans so as not to cause trouble for Maire as she settled into her new wedded life with Duncan FitzWilliam. There had been some grumbling when Ronan had made that surprising announcement to his clansmen, but the stronghold's storehouses were full of provisions and cattle grazed in the pastures while game aplenty roamed the hills.

Triona knew that in time the raids would begin anew, so she cherished every moment of Ronan being home with her and Deirdre instead of riding hard through the woods to attack a Norman settlement. Especially sweet moments like these when one bout of lovemaking this night would soon lead to another, her cheeks flushing hot with anticipation.

Although married for two years with one wee daughter and another babe due in seven months' time, she and Ronan shared a blazing hunger for each other that never failed to take her breath away. Their love burned so brightly between them...a deep unbreakable bond that she hoped Niall would find one day—

"Enough of my brother, woman." As if he'd read her mind, Ronan's husky whisper thrilled Triona to her toes as he gathered her closer against him. "In time Niall will find another beautiful blonde to capture his heart...though I swear when he returns, he'll have much to answer for to have worried us so—"

"Kiss me, Ronan." Triona didn't wait for him, but pressed her lips to his as she felt his tension rising again over Niall. She sighed against the warmth of Ronan's mouth and teased him with the tip of her tongue, and whooped with delight as he rolled over onto his back suddenly and pulled her with him.

Now she lay atop the length of him, a rock hard bulge pressing at the heart of her thighs, a lusty look on his handsome face as she raked her fingers through his midnight hair. With a low intake of breath he shifted his hips and then she felt him thrust slowly into her, filling her, his strong hands cupping her bottom to draw her closer.

Everything fell away but the cool night breeze wafting through the window and the bright moonlight spilling across the floor...as he stared into her eyes and rocked her into sweet, heavenly oblivion.

***

Ostmentown, Ireland

"Oh, God." With a groan, Niall O'Byrne rolled onto his back upon the dock and stared at the brilliant full moon shining down upon him.

Mocking him. Laughing at him. The cold heartless orb daring him to raise the wineskin to his mouth for another swallow…although Niall was so drunk that he doubted he could lift his arm.

He'd been drunk for two months and this night was no different.

The same dock. The same raucous laughter from the riverside tavern that he'd stumbled out of only moments before. Or was it an hour past now? Who could say? All he knew was that these wild-haired Ostmen could drink more than any men he'd ever known, although he'd done his very best to keep up with them.

Sleep like the dead all day, choke down enough food to stay alive, and then drink long into the night until he passed out again upon the dock where he lay now, tormented by visions of Caitlin MacMurrough.

Damn her, why would she not leave him in peace? With ships from countless ports lined up along the dock and the dark water of the River Liffey coursing beneath him, Niall squinted against the moonlight.

Why did the silvery beams have to remind him so torturously of her long blond hair that had once slipped like silk between his fingers? Why could he not forget the incredible emerald green of her eyes? The softness of her skin? The beauty of her smile? Her sweet laughter? Her kiss...ah, God, her kiss! Damn it all, he clearly wasn't drunk enough yet!

Now Niall lifted the wineskin above him to squeeze the tart liquid into his mouth, though he missed and sprayed his bearded face and the front of his tunic. Cursing under his breath, he used his thumb to wipe droplets of wine from his ear and then attempted to sit up—only to collapse back onto the dock.

Aye, perhaps that merciful oblivion where he felt nothing, remembered nothing, was closing in upon him after all. He shut his eyes against the relentless moonlight and the taunting visions of Caitlin, his beloved Caitlin—no, the treacherous and fickle Caitlin!

"Damn all women," Niall muttered, rolling with effort onto his side. "Damn them to hell—what the devil?"

He had felt the sharp kick to his shin even as he heard a piercing shriek. Grimacing in pain, he glanced up to see a wild flash of white fly past him.

Fly past him with arms flailing as the screeching apparition toppled headfirst from the dock and into the River Liffey, splashing Niall with cold water.

This time he did sit up, but he heard nothing. Only silence. Had he imagined that someone had just fallen into the river?

Then Niall saw it, a slim white arm in the moonlight breaking through the surface as if grabbing for something, anything to hold onto even as a desperate cry burst from the woman's throat.

"Help me! Please!"

She disappeared as suddenly, her head and then her arm slipping between the lapping water even as Niall hauled himself to his feet. He didn't think, he didn't blink, but dove into the river at the spot where he'd just seen the woman sink below the surface.

Wildly he spun underwater, but he felt nothing, could see nothing. Had she already been carried downstream? His lungs bursting, he dove deeper instead and then caught a handful of hair. He tugged upward and grabbed the woman beneath the arms, her body limp against him.

The river seemed a live thing sweeping them along in the current, threatening to drag both of them down into the cold black depths. With all the strength he possessed, Niall kicked upward powerfully and broke through the surface, gasping for breath even as the woman seemed not to breathe at all.

He could but swim with her to the shore, the moonlight a bright beacon as his feet found bottom and he swept the woman up into his arms. Within an instant he had hauled her out onto the muddy bank where he laid her down and rolled her onto her side.

Relief filled him to see that she was breathing, barely. He pounded her back once, twice, and then she coughed and sputtered, her thick wet hair covering her face.

No wonder she had sunk like a rock, what with the heavy cloak she had wound around her, a white garment underneath clinging to her like a second skin. He saw then a thin glistening of gold at her wrist, a leather pouch lying in the mud. He leaned over her to wipe sodden hair from her face, but she pushed away from him and struggled back toward the water.

"No, please, leave me! Let me die. Let me die!"

"Woman, are you mad? One moment you cry for help and then the next you crawl for the river? I nearly drowned to save you!"

Niall shook her, hard, and she stopped struggling only to stare up into his face as if seeing him for the first time. He stared back into her eyes, great limpid pools in the glaring moonlight of what color he could not fathom—until suddenly she pulled away from him and curled up into a shivering ball in the mud and weeds.

Great sobs began to shake her as she wept piteously, while Niall could only stare at her in confusion and shake his head.

One thing he knew for certain. If he'd been falling down drunk only moments before, now he was stone-cold sober.

CHAPTER 2

"Easy now, easy," Niall said above her sobs in an attempt to soothe her. "You've had a terrible shock."

He reached out to touch the woman's shoulder, but she jerked away from him and tucked herself more tightly into a ball. He had never heard such weeping…as if her heart was breaking.

But why? That she had survived and not drowned? He could see in the moonlight that she was a young woman, perhaps no more than eighteen or nineteen years, and well-dressed from the quality of the cloak that had nearly sealed her doom.

What had she been doing out alone on the dock? There were women aplenty at the tavern eager to satisfy the sexual needs of the rowdy Ostmen, whose appetite for drinking was second only to their lust for whoring. Yet this woman was no such creature, Niall sensed as clearly as he'd begun to shiver himself.

He felt chilled to the bone, the muck squishing beneath

them only making matters worse. They needed a warm fire and blankets, and fast. He didn't need daylight to see that she quaked from head to toe from her wet clothing, her lips turning blue.

"Come on, we can't stay here." He said no more but gathered her into his arms, and this time she didn't flinch away from him. Didn't fight him. Instead she went limp against him, which made him certain his instincts were correct.

The river might not have claimed her, but if they didn't find warmth soon the chill would end her life as surely as drowning. As he rose to his feet, swaying to find his footing in the mud, she stared up at him through half opened eyes.

Tears glistened in the corners and streaked her face, her skin as white as death as she mouthed words that held no sound.

She looked so innocent.

So lost.

So hopeless. Niall felt a sudden catch in his throat. He clutched her slender body more tightly against him as a powerful wave of protectiveness surged through him.

Jesu, Mary, and Joseph, why had she begged him to let her die? She had been running along the dock—mayhap fleeing something or someone that clearly terrified her—until she had tripped over his leg and tumbled into the river. Niall swore then and there to himself that *no one* would hurt this hapless woman while he had anything to say about it.

"I'm not going to hurt you, I promise. I need to get you warm."

She said nothing, her head lolling against his shoulder, and Niall knew then she was barely conscious. He glanced up the shoreline at the ships along the dock, the sounds of carousing carrying to him from the distance. He wasn't surprised that the fierce current had carried them so far from the more populated area of Ostmentown, which made it all the more a miracle that they had both survived.

He looked across the river at the towering walls surrounding Dublin, the battlements lit by torches and guarded by Norman soldiers.

Accursed bastards! For two months he had been only a river crossing away from the O'Byrne clan's most hated enemies, and he'd learned from the Ostmen that they despised the Normans as well. Yet for some reason the Ostmen and the Normans obeyed an unspoken rule that they each stick to their own side of the River Liffey, which had given Niall the refuge he'd needed among these seafaring people who were as native to Éire as the Irish.

No one had questioned his presence among them and he doubted they would now either, but for the woman he bore in his arms. No, he couldn't return to the tavern. He needed a quieter place, a safer place…

A glance to the east and Niall saw it then, a small stone church flanked by a stable and other outbuildings. Holding the woman close, he cleared the mud along the riverbank and set off with long strides through the tall grass toward the church. He felt warmed at once by his exertion but the woman still shivered uncontrollably, which alarmed him.

God help him, was she willing herself to die? He quickened his pace, and when at last he came to the church he didn't bother to knock but gave a thunderous kick to the front door. It didn't take long for the dim light beneath the door to grow brighter, someone approaching with shuffling steps.

"Open the door! This woman needs help!" Niall shouted, although he could already hear a heavy bolt being withdrawn inside. It didn't surprise him that the church would be locked against intruders with all the foreign ships plying the River Liffey, but this humble place surely had little to plunder.

Golden light from a guttering lantern spilled out into the night as the door was opened by a wizened old priest with great owlish eyes who studied Niall warily. "Help, you say?"

"Aye, this woman nearly drowned. I saved her, but she needs a bed, a fire, warm blankets—dammit, will you watch her breathe her last at the church door?" Niall didn't wait for an answer, but pushed past the priest into the small narthex. "I'm no thief and wish you no harm. If it's coin you need, I can supply it. Where do you sleep, Priest?"

As if he had suddenly grasped the gravity of the situation, the old man glanced with apology from Niall to the woman in his arms. "This way, forgive me. No coin is needed." Quickly he shut the church door and drew the bolt, then indicated for Niall to follow him.

Niall obliged as the priest held the lantern high and led

them down the aisle toward the simple altar graced by golden candlesticks and an ornate gold cross with a blood-red ruby at the center.

Not so humble after all, Niall thought with some surprise when the priest turned to the left and led the way through an arched doorway into an adjoining building constructed of matching stone. A low fire burned in the central hearth, a cot pulled close where clearly the priest must have been dozing when Niall had pounded upon the door.

At once Niall rushed to the fire and laid the woman upon the cot, and quickly removed her sodden cloak. A sharp gasp behind him made Niall glance at the priest, who had turned away at the sight of the woman dressed only in what Niall realized now was a white sleeping gown.

A soaked sleeping gown of fine linen that clung to her full breasts, her narrow waist and shapely hips, her rosy nipples pressed taut against the gossamer fabric and a dusky triangular shadow between her thighs...

"Blankets, man, we need blankets!" Niall swallowed hard and focused on the task at hand, immediately stripping the woman of her wet sleeping gown and covering her at once with a thin scratchy blanket the priest had offered to him. "Surely you have more?"

The old man nodded and disappeared through a narrow door off to one side, emerging a moment later with several blankets of fine soft wool. Again, he appeared apologetic.

"My brother priest Gilbert's chamber. He's away for a

wedding. Lord MacTorkil's stronghold in Ostmentown—but I'm sure he won't mind…the use of his blankets, I mean."

Niall didn't say a word, his jaw tight as he replaced the thin blanket with the fine thick ones that he wrapped snugly around the woman. Only then did he rise to stoke the fire smoldering in the hearth until the flames crackled brightly and welcome heat emanated around them.

Relief filled him to see that the woman's cheeks held color now, her lips no longer blue but a soft pink hue. He accepted the chair the priest had brought him and sat down beside the cot, staring at her.

At the richly embroidered cloak lying in a steaming clump upon the stone floor.

At the discarded sleeping gown as fine as those he and Ronan had taken during raids upon wealthy Norman lords and ladies to give to Triona, his sister Maire, and other women of their clan.

At the muddy leather bag still dangling from the woman's wrist, though Niall was not inclined to discover its contents.

He had already sensed much about this unfortunate woman, though she had yet to open her eyes or utter another word.

She lay so still, but she breathed steadily now. Her thick auburn hair that appeared waist-length was no longer sodden but drying in soft tendrils around her face.

She was no beauty, aye, and some might even call her almost plain, but her skin was soft and smooth and the color of cream. Her hands lovely, her fingers long and slim and showing no hint of toil.

Whoever she was, this young woman had never known a day's work in her life but only one of wealth and privilege—

"M-my lord?"

Niall glanced at the old priest, who held out a wooden plate laden with bread, cheese, and a slice of salted meat. "I am no lord. Just a traveler."

"Aye, of course, but you must be hungry…and thirsty as well. I've freshly brewed ale—"

"No ale," Niall said, still amazed that after all the wine he'd consumed that night, he felt so clearheaded. Yet he supposed that nearly drowning could do that to a man. Then he thought better of the priest's offer, not for himself, but for the woman. She probably could use a sip or two of something bracing. "Aye, bring the ale…and my thanks."

With a humble nod, the priest retreated while Niall set the plate of food upon a low stool. In truth he wasn't hungry, so he would save the meal for the woman. As for the rest of him, his tunic and trousers were almost dry and his knife thankfully not lost to the river but still sheathed at his belt. His brown leather boots were soaked through and perhaps ruined, though. With a resigned shrug, Niall tugged off first one boot and then the other and set them next to the hearth to dry.

There was nothing else to do but sit…and wait. Niall stared into the flames as he ran his hand through his damp hair and wondered what he was going to do next with this woman whose life he'd saved.

A woman who had begged at first for help and then begged to die, as if by sinking into the river's depths all hope had sunk as well within her.

Yet he had known his own despair these past two months, drinking himself into a stupor each night to attempt to escape his anger, hurt, and a stabbing pain in his heart that never seemed to leave him—

"Ale, my lord."

Niall sighed heavily as he glanced over his shoulder. He took the cup from the priest, not wooden or pewter but brightly polished silver. "Your brother priest's cup?"

"Aye. Father Gilbert is a well-born man and enjoys some finer things around him, though I bear it as no sin. He's long been a priest to the MacTorkil clan. He left only this morning to officiate tomorrow at the wedding of Lord MacTorkil's daughter to a man come all the way from Norway to have her—"

"No..."

The sound had been no more than a whisper. Niall turned around to find the woman staring at first him and then the priest as if they had both grown two heads and meant to devour her.

Staring at them with eyes as beautiful and brilliant a blue as any Niall had seen...and widened with fright.

"No!"

Her outcry ringing in the room, she flung aside the blankets and vaulted suddenly from the cot. Niall nearly toppled from the chair, the ale cup clattering to the floor, when she shoved against him to add momentum to her flight.

Her long tousled hair flying behind her, she fled naked toward the door while the priest stumbled out of the way and crossed himself.

Doused with ale, Niall lunged after her. She was fast, but he was faster. He caught her in his arms just before she reached the door.

"No! Let me go! Let me go!"

He'd thought she had fought him before, but now she kicked and flailed and struggled in his arms as if possessed. Her shrieks were shrill, terrified.

"Woman, I told you I wouldn't hurt you!" Niall countered as he carried her back to the cot. "You're safe here, I swear it. By God, I swear it!"

As if his words had seared into her brain, she ceased her struggles and fought him no more as Niall laid her on the cot and covered her with the blankets. Either that or she had simply exhausted herself as she stared at him with those incredible blue eyes now filling with tears.

Swallowing hard, Niall doubted he had ever seen a more wretched sight…and he felt more determined than ever to discover what lay at the heart of her distress.

"Leave us, Priest!" he commanded over his shoulder, not taking his gaze from her face. Nor did she take her gaze from his face as if truly seeing him for the very first time.

The door closed behind the priest, leaving Niall and the woman alone. He drew the chair close to the cot and sat down beside her, and kept his voice low.

"I want to help you, woman, but first you must tell me your name. Who are you?"

CHAPTER 3

Tell him her name? This stranger who had saved her
from drowning and sworn that she was safe? That
he would not hurt her?

Uncertain of what to do, Nora could only stare at him
silently as hot tears blurred her vision. Yet she still could
see that his blue-gray eyes were kind and filled with
concern.

That his face was handsome in spite of a bushy,
unkempt beard, his dark brown hair long at the neck and
glinting with red in the firelight.

That his chest and shoulders were so broad…and she'd
already felt the powerful strength of his arms when he'd
carried her from the river and just now back to the cot.

How could she have come upon such a man? She
recalled running in desperation along the dock, trying to
choose a ship where she might find refuge. A ship that
would hopefully sail at first light and take her far away from
Sigurd Skullcrusher and a marriage that would spell her
doom.

Too late she had spied someone lying flat out on the dock and she had tripped over him, falling headlong into the river.

Nora grimaced as she recalled the water's icy chill, her heavy cloak dragging her down, down into the black depths…

"Whoa, now, it cannot be as bad as all that," came a low, teasing voice as Nora met again the stranger's eyes to find him smiling at her reassuringly. "You're warm here by the fire…and there's food and ale if you wish it—"

"Was that you on the dock? I-I tripped—"

"Aye, it was me." He had sobered suddenly, though his gaze was still kind. "Forgive me. It wasn't my intent that you should take a moonlit swim. Nor myself for that matter, but what could I do? You cried out for help…well, at first you did. I couldn't let you drown—"

"I wish you had." Overcome with despair, Nora closed her eyes against fresh, burning tears and turned her face away from him. "You cannot help me. No one can help me."

He didn't answer, but fell silent except for a heavy sigh. Nora started when she suddenly felt his fingers at her chin as he gently turned her back to face him. He looked so serious, any humor she'd seen in his eyes moments ago all but fled.

"I understand. I'm a stranger to you, asking your name when you've no idea whether you can trust me. You were running from something—someone. I swore after I carried you from the river that no one would hurt you, and I swear it to you now, as surely as my name is Niall O'Byrne."

She blinked at him, recognizing at once a rebel clan name that had become legendary in Éire.

The O'Byrnes' raids upon the invading Normans were the stuff of admiring tales told in her father's great hall, the Ostmen longing for the day when they regained power enough to rise up as well against that hated enemy. Yet now by running away from a marriage arranged to achieve that very end, she had thwarted her own people—no, she would not think of it!

"Tell me no more," she said softly, knowing he had revealed much in just his name. "The priest might hear you—"

"Let him hear. I would have you trust me...so now you've my life in your hands. As Tanist to my brother, Ronan Black O'Byrne, chieftain of the Glenmalure O'Byrnes, I've a price on my head triple my weight in gold. Those bastard Normans across the river would love nothing more than to see me hang from the highest tower of Dublin Castle—"

"No, please, you must not tell me anything more!" Without thinking, Nora reached up and pressed her fingers to his lips to silence him. His mouth was warm, his breath upon her fingertips strangely moving her. She had never touched any man before. He reached up and removed her fingers from his lips only to encompass them in a hand so much larger than her own.

A strong hand. His palm rough and callused no doubt from wielding a sword against a hated enemy to Irish and

Ostmen alike. His gaze hadn't left hers and now he leaned closer, intently staring into her eyes.

"Woman, I would know your name."

"Nora," she breathed, feeling suddenly unable to help herself. "Nora MacTorkil."

"*Nora MacTorkil?*" came the priest's astonished cry from across the room. He stood as if rooted to the floor, a fresh cup of ale in his hand. "Daughter to Lord Magnus MacTorkil? Why…why you're to wed tomorrow—ah, lord, please don't kill me!"

It had happened so fast that Nora could only gape as Niall had lunged from his chair to rush over and press his knife to the old priest's throat.

"I told you to leave us, Priest."

"I-I did, but you had spilled your ale, lord! I thought you might want more…if not for yourself, then for the esteemed lady—oh, God help me."

Esteemed lady. A terrible ache in the pit of her stomach, Nora thought for an instant she might be sick. The priest had recognized her name and knew who she was. All was lost. *All was lost!*

She could but watch, stricken, as Niall grabbed the priest by the collar of his brown robe and hauled him over to the chair, where he pushed him down into the seat.

"Who was she to wed?" Niall demanded, the knife now pressed beneath the priest's chin while Nora felt the color draining from her face.

"Sigurd Knutson, lord! A great warrior come from the north with eight shiploads of his men. Father Gilbert could speak of nothing else this past week, such was his excitement. The MacTorkil's daughter Nora marrying into the royal house of Norway—a great alliance for the Ostmen!"

Certain now she might retch, Nora still felt pity for the terrified old man as a thin trickle of blood seeped from the knifepoint piercing his flesh. She glanced up at Niall, whose expression looked so hard now in the flickering firelight. He stood so tall above them, so formidable, appearing every inch a rebel O'Byrne to be dreaded and feared.

"Please...don't hurt him," she said barely above a whisper, and to her relief Niall at once lowered his knife. He still held fast to the priest's collar, though, as if he sensed the old man might try to escape at the first opportunity.

"You fled from this man...this Sigurd Knutson?" came Niall's low query as he seemed to study her face.

Nora nodded, seeing no reason to tell him anything but the truth. Now it seemed her life was in his hands as well. Somehow she formed the words that stuck like bile in her throat. "Not a man. A monster. He's buried four wives already. Kills men with his bare hands. They call him Skullcrusher."

The room fell silent but for the priest's nervous breathing and the sputtering of flames, though Nora could swear her pounding heart drowned out all else.

Why was Niall looking at her so intently...as if weighing something in his mind? Yet in the next instant the priest cried out in surprise as Niall suddenly yanked him to his feet.

"Old man, I wish you no harm, but you must swear to me now that you'll speak of this night to no one. Not to your Father Gilbert, nor anyone who might question you if you've seen this woman. No one! Are we understood?"

"Aye, lord, not a word!" said the priest, sweat beading his wrinkled brow.

"Swear it!"

"Aye, I swear!"

"Good, now we must leave this place."

"Leave?" Staring up at Niall in confusion, Nora clutched the blankets to her breast. "Where?"

Niall didn't answer, instead pulling on his boots and then barking orders at the priest. "She needs clothing, an extra robe if you have one. And a bag of food. Move, man!"

As the priest hastened to obey, Nora watched Niall gather up her cloak and sleeping gown from the floor and tie them into a bundle.

"Your garments are still damp, and I don't want you catching a chill."

"Chill?" she asked dumbly.

"The night air. If your absence has been discovered, they'll already be looking for you. We can't stay here."

Terror filled her at the thought of Sigurd Skullcrusher crashing around her father's stronghold to find her. Nora was only too glad to see the priest rush forward with a brown robe like the one he wore.

"Put it on, Nora, quickly," came Niall's command and

she didn't waste a moment. Giving no thought to her nakedness, she rose from the cot and took the garment from the priest, who averted his eyes.

"It's too large for you, my lady, but Father Gilbert is a stout man."

"My thanks, Father…"

"Edmund, my lady. Father Edmund."

"I will not forget your kindness," she murmured, drawing the plain woolen garment over her head and her arms through the long sleeves. The leather pouch at her wrist caught in the one sleeve, but she tugged it through. She glanced at Niall. He appeared satisfied with her garb once she tied a rope belt around her waist, though he had been pacing impatiently.

"The food, man! Have you horses in the stable?"

"One, a sturdy beast though long in years. Father Gilbert—"

"I know, I know," came Niall's wry reply. "He took the better one."

"Aye, lord, so he did."

As the priest hastened off again to fetch the food, Nora looked down at her bare feet. She realized for the first time that she must have lost her leather slippers in the river.

"We'll be riding, not walking," Niall reassured her, taking her hand to draw her with him from the room.

She remembered little of when they had arrived, mayhap a glimpse of gold. She realized, too, when they entered the sanctuary that she must have seen the candlesticks and cross upon the altar. Instead of leading her into the narthex to await the bag of food from the priest, Niall led her toward that same altar as Nora glanced up at him in confusion.

"Do you trust me, Nora MacTorkil?" he asked her quietly, dropping the bundle of clothing he carried upon the stone floor. He turned to face her so he could take her hands in his.

"Aye," she said simply, though she had no idea where he might be taking her or what he now had in mind. "I trust you, Niall O'Byrne."

"Over here!" Niall called to the priest, who had hurried into the sanctuary and turned toward the narthex. Appearing as startled as Nora to find them instead at the altar, Father Edmund rushed forward.

"My lord?"

"You will marry us here, *now*, Priest, and make it the fastest vows you've ever uttered."

Marry? So stunned that she felt her knees give way beneath her, Nora was grateful that Niall held her fast so she would not fall.

He continued to hold her fast as the priest hastily led them through vows that seemed over before they had begun. Nora's soft "Aye" was barely above a whisper when Father Edmund asked if she would take Niall O'Byrne for her husband.

Then the lightning-fast ceremony was done. Niall led her with one hand toward the front of the church, while he carried her bundled clothing and the bag of food in the other. Only at the door did he stop to look down at her, while she could but stare up at him in complete amazement.

"I said I would help you, and now the thing is done. You've nothing to fear any longer from Sigurd Knutson. You're my bride, Nora O'Byrne. I dare any man to take you from me."

CHAPTER 4

Niall stared at the descending full moon, grateful for the sturdy gelding beneath him and Nora that had carried them this far into Wicklow.

His bride, Nora.

God in heaven, had he really taken a wife this night? It seemed one moment he had been lying drunk upon a dock and now he had become the husband to Lord Magnus MacTorkil's own daughter—and him one of the richest merchants in all of Éire!

Not that Niall cared one whit for the man's wealth, which in truth meant nothing to him. Yet such riches could buy trouble down the road if Father Edmund failed to hold his tongue, though Niall had sensed a goodness in the man that would make him likely to honor his oath. Jesu, Mary, and Joseph, may that old priest honor his oath!

These thoughts and so many others had plagued Niall since they had left the church, skirting first around Ostmentown and then heading south through wooded hills toward the O'Byrnes' domain in the Wicklow Mountains.

Fortunately the night had remained clear, the moon lighting their way through the trees as they traveled well off the beaten path. The sounds of the night were all around them…a hooting owl, a wolf howling, as well as the gelding's hooves thudding upon the earth. He had heard, too, an occasional sigh from Nora, who rode astride the horse with her arms around Niall's waist and her head resting against his back.

She hadn't said a word during the journey, and he knew exhaustion had overtaken her when he'd felt her arms go lax. He'd kept one hand on the reins and his free hand clasping her leg so she wouldn't fall from their mount…while the gravity of what he'd done had run over and over through his mind.

First and foremost, he didn't love her. He would love no woman ever again. What had that useless emotion brought him but heartache and regret?

For two long years he had waited for Caitlin MacMurrough at the behest of her father until she reached eighteen years, and much good it had done him. He had sworn his love for her and she her love for him time and again…and yet Caitlin had chosen another man to wed! A godson of Donal MacMurrough's named Brian!

Niall grunted his disgust. God help him if he ever came face-to-face with that bastard who had stolen his bride. Aye, he wasn't so cruel as to make Caitlin a widow, but her husband would look none the better for all the bruises once Niall was done thrashing him.

"Oh!"

Nora's pained cry made Niall realize with a start how forcefully he had been gripping her arms, so furious had been his musings. Doing his best to shove any thought of Caitlin from his mind, he slowed the gelding's steady trot to a walk. They still had several hours' ride ahead of them to reach Ronan's stronghold in Glenmalure, but Niall doubted Nora could endure much more traveling this night.

Besides, there was an important matter to attend to before the sun rose upon their first day together as husband and wife…

"Forgive me, Nora, I held you too tightly," he said over his shoulder, and felt her small nod against him. "There's an abandoned settlement over the rise where we'll stop and rest for a few hours. Normans once lived there until my brother Ronan and our clansmen chased them off O'Byrne lands. If they're wise they won't dare to return, the thieving bastards."

Again he felt her nod, the side of her face pressed against his back, and he knew he'd made the right decision.

From the gently-bred looks of her, she had probably never spent so much time before atop a horse. He had seen her in terrible distress earlier that night, aye, but now her quiet temperament reminded him of his sister Maire, who also weighed heavily upon his mind.

What had become of her in the two months since he'd rode away from Glenmalure after letting her know that the man she loved, Lord Duncan FitzWilliam, though grievously wounded, still lived? More troubling, Niall could well imagine Ronan's fury had not abated that his beloved younger sister had fallen in love with a Norman.

Niall hated the merciless invaders as much as his brother, but Duncan FitzWilliam had shown himself to be a rare man, an honorable man in a land torn apart by so much strife and bloodshed between Irish and Norman. Had he fully recovered from his wound? Had he attempted to send word to Maire that all was not lost for them?

Niall sent a silent prayer heavenward that his sweet sister was well, and that somehow there might be a way for her and the baron who had won her heart to be reunited.

Ronan, of course, would do anything in his power to keep them apart, but he hadn't turned his fiery-haired wife Triona away when he learned that Norman blood ran in her veins. Their little daughter Deirdre had Norman blood in her veins! Aye, if Niall's fierce, stubborn brother had been moved out of love, then surely there was hope for Maire.

For the first time in weeks feeling eager to be home again, Niall found himself wishing that he and Nora could ride on but resisted the impulse. He felt her arms trembling around him, and knew the strain of their flight from Ostmentown had taxed her greatly.

"We're almost there, wife. Take heart." Niall kicked the gelding into a trot again and felt Nora's arms tighten around his waist, though she still trembled.

Wife. Oddly enough, the word hadn't sounded so strange upon his tongue, which surprised him.

Aye, in the eyes of the Church and before God, she was his wife, but not in all ways.

Not yet.

She wouldn't truly be considered his lawful bride until the deed was done…and soon.

Wife. Nora pressed her face against Niall's back and held on to him tightly, breathing in his masculine scent. Sweat, a hint of the river, a tinge of ale, and something that must be uniquely his own that she found strangely stirring. He felt so warm through his clothing, too, that she'd felt no need for a cloak even if hers hadn't been wet and useless and stuffed into a saddlebag.

How could she have imagined that a man this close could smell so appealing and radiate such warmth? She'd never ridden atop a horse hugging a man before…yet Niall O'Byrne wasn't just any man. He was her husband and he had just called her 'wife'!

Husband. How had this miracle come to be? Even when dozing from exhaustion, she had been enveloped in a state of wonderment.

She was no longer a MacTorkil, but an O'Byrne bride! Earlier that evening she had been distraught and beside herself, fleeing for her life into the night only to stumble over this man who had rescued her.

Married her.

Escaped with her deep into the Wicklow hills where fierce rebel clans ruled and their enemies feared to venture if they valued their lives.

Aye, she trusted Niall O'Byrne implicitly. She had told

him so in the church and now she felt that trust resonate in every fiber of her being. How could she not? He had saved her life...and given her a new one. A life she had never expected or dreamed of and that had only just begun.

Well...not yet fully begun. The thought made her tremble anew, and not from the coolness of the night air.

Soon they would stop for a few hours. To rest, Niall had said. That meant they would lie down somewhere together...as husband and wife. To sleep, or perhaps not to sleep—

"We're here, Nora. Wait for me while I make sure all is safe."

He dismounted before she could answer, his tone filled with low command that she had no thought to disregard.

She watched him, captivated, as he disappeared stealthily through an opening in a shattered palisade that must have once guarded this Norman settlement until the O'Byrnes had reclaimed it. She felt a chill, imagining the screams of terror, women wailing, children crying, and the wild whoops of the rebel Irish as they overran what to these foolish people must have deemed impregnable.

An owl screeched above her, which made Nora start.

She glanced around her, not liking at all being left alone though she doubted Niall would have done so if he'd truly felt there was danger. As long moments passed, she thanked God for the moonlight, which filtered through the thick branches and lent an otherworldly glow around her.

The full moon she had cursed earlier for its brightness had, like a welcome presence, guided their way to safety this night. She knew only a few more hours and the sun would rise, which left very little time for sleep—oh, why could she not stop trembling?

Nora took a deep, shuddering breath as Niall reappeared suddenly and took the reins to lead their mount into the enclosure. She could see several dwelling-houses and a cluster of smaller outbuildings, but he stopped at the nearest structure and tethered the gelding to a post. Without a word, he reached up and his hands encircled her waist to lift her to the ground.

Yet to her surprise, he didn't readily release her. His strong hands lingered at her waist, while Nora was certain she'd never felt her heart leap so against her breast.

"I've lit a fire in the hearth. Go in while I draw water from the well…and take the bag of food. I'll follow soon."

Nora nodded, struck dumb. Could such simple words have flustered her more completely? He handed her the bag, his fingers brushing hers, and she jumped.

Oh dear, why had it suddenly become so difficult to breathe? If he had noticed how disconcerted she'd become, she didn't read it in his face. He looked at her steadily and gave her a gentle nudge.

"Go on. You've nothing to fear, Nora. All is well."

Again she nodded, not knowing what else to do but oblige him. Yet just before she stepped inside the dwelling-house, she glanced over her shoulder to see him leading the horse toward what must be a stable.

She could not deny that his care for the exhausted beast moved her, which spoke even more to the character of this man she had wed. A stranger to her only hours ago, but now who soon might share her bed—

"Oh God."

She fairly ran into the dwelling-house, but came up short once inside.

A warming fire indeed burned brightly in the central hearth, a pale blue cloth freshly draped over a table, and the floor clearly swept in haste from the swirls of dust marking the planked floor.

Incredibly, Nora smiled for the first time in what seemed like days.

Had Niall truly left her waiting outside the settlement to see that it was safe, or to attempt to make things more comfortable for her?

A little of both, she imagined, undeniably touched by the effort he'd made on her behalf…and amused, too. She felt a giggle welling in her throat, and her laughter burst forth as she imagined this tall handsome rebel wielding not a sword, but a broom!

"You should do that more often, Nora."

She spun, startled to find Niall staring at her from the doorway where he set a bucket of water at his feet.

"Laugh. Smile. You've a beautiful smile."

He smiled now at her, too, and if Nora had thought him handsome before, even with his beard, now she doubted she had ever seen a man more striking to look upon. She brought her hand to her mouth, tears filling her eyes.

No one…absolutely *no one* had told her she had a

beautiful smile other than her twin sister Kristina, whom Nora had loved so dearly. And now this man…her husband of only a few hours—

"Nora, forgive me."

Nora gulped back a sob as Niall rushed to her side, his expression filled with concern.

"What have I said to distress you so? Tell me."

Another sob bursting forth, Nora could not say a word, only shaking her head. At once Niall took the bag of food from her and led her to a stool, which she sank onto gratefully.

All her life she had been called passing fair, or plain, and she had grown used to it and never expected anything different.

Even Sigurd Skullcrusher had mocked her when he'd first seen her, roaring out to everyone in her father's hall that she didn't need to be beautiful to bear him sons, as long as her hips were full and rounded. How Sigurd's men had jeered and hooted while she had simply wanted to melt into the floor—

"Nora."

She felt Niall lift her chin to look at him, and she realized he had sunk to his one knee beside her. Tears welling in her eyes, she could but look at him and whisper brokenly, "This…is a dream. It has to be…"

CHAPTER 5

Niall felt a catch in his throat, never having felt more moved as he stared into Nora's lovely blue eyes.

Blue as the sea with tiny flecks of gold like sunlight. Yet filled with tears as if her heart were breaking, and it didn't take much for him to reason why.

A virgin. An innocent. With this their wedding night, she must be frightened...

"No dream, Nora, and I pray you don't think it a nightmare—"

"No, no, I did not mean..." She didn't finish, but appeared to swallow her tears as she brushed the back of her hand across her eyes. She seemed to smile then with embarrassment, sniffling, and met his gaze. "I had thought I wanted to die...and then you saved me. Married me to protect me. And me a stranger to you—"

"No stranger now, but my wife. We've a lifetime to learn about each other...starting tonight."

There. He'd said it, Niall thought, gauging her response

though she simply stared back at him and nodded. She must know that as husband and wife now, they must consummate their marriage…and given the circumstances, the sooner, the better. Finding himself drawn again to the uncommon beauty of her gaze, he cleared his throat and rose to his feet.

Another woman's gaze had once drawn him so, Caitlin's, though her eyes were a deep emerald green. Just a glance from her had made him weak in the knees like a besotted fool—damn it all, he would not think of her!

Especially not this night with his new bride looking up at him with trust shining in her eyes that undeniably moved him, too. What the devil was coming over him? He didn't want to be made weak in the knees or stirred so by the gaze of any woman ever again!

Niall abruptly left her side and tossed the bag of food upon the table. He jerked his head toward a side door as he pulled out a round loaf of bread, a wedge of cheese, and strips of salted meat.

"An outhouse lies beyond that door. I've lit a lantern there so you may see to your needs." He'd spoken more gruffly than he should have, but couldn't seem to help himself as he sensed her movement behind him. "Ronan and I use this place when hunting, so it isn't entirely lacking in comfort. Just dusty. When you return, I'll have a bowl of water for you in the sleeping room if you wish to bathe."

He heard her murmured thanks, and a soft thud as she passed by him and placed the leather pouch she'd worn around her wrist upon the table. Flecked with dried mud from the riverbank and water-stained, the pouch was a stark reminder of the terror and anguish Nora had suffered, which only made Niall angrier at himself.

Caitlin's treachery was none of Nora's doing! By God, when would these wretched memories of the woman who had broken his heart leave him in peace?

With a low curse, Niall focused on the tasks at hand, determined to speak only kindly to Nora from then on and to put her as much at ease as possible.

Some moments later when he heard the creaking door as Nora came back inside, he was finished with his efforts to make things comfortable for her.

The fire in the hearth stoked against the night's chill.

A bowl of water with a soft cloth awaiting her in the adjoining sleeping room.

The blanket upon the bed shaken outside and then draped back over the lumpy mattress.

Anything fine or valuable left by the fleeing Normans had long since been taken as plunder back to Glenmalure, so he'd done the best he could for their wedding night. As Nora wordlessly came toward him, her eyes wide and luminous in the firelight, Niall gestured to the table.

"Come and sit. You must be hungry—"

"I-I'm not really. If you don't mind, I'll wait for you...I mean, in the other room..."

She faltered, clearly nervous from the way she fidgeted with the rope belt at her waist as she glanced toward the sleeping room and then back to Niall. He saw the anxiousness in her gaze and he sought at once to reassure her.

"You've nothing to fear, Nora O'Byrne. I'll not hurt you…never hurt you."

She nodded, gave him a tremulous smile, and then fairly fled to the adjoining room before Niall could utter another word.

Where was he? Nora wondered.

Her heart beating fiercely against her breast, she pulled the musty-smelling blanket up to her chin and stared at the strip of light from the doorway.

She had heard Niall moving around in the other room for what had seemed an eternity to her, though she couldn't really say how much time had passed.

Not long after she had run into the sleeping room and closed the door but for a few inches, she had heard him stoking the fire. She had never stripped so fast and bathed herself, believing he might join her at any moment and not wanting to be found standing stark naked at the wash bowl. She had done her best to work her fingers quickly through her long tangled hair, but had given up for lack of a comb. Then she had jumped into the bed, barely wide enough for two, and coughed at the puff of dust emanating from the worn mattress.

In truth, she had never slept before on anything so rustic, though she had felt touched again by the neatly draped blanket and hastily swept floor. Niall's efforts to make her comfortable were so kind and caring, how could she not be moved?

Such gratitude had overwhelmed her as she lay there waiting for him, that to her the room had transformed into the most magnificent bower. Yet she couldn't deny that breathless nervousness had swept her, too, every time she heard sounds coming from the adjoining room.

The scraping of a chair as he must have sat at the table for a few moments to eat.

His footfalls upon the floor until she had heard him kick off his boots.

The sound of water splashing in a bowl as he, too, was taking the time to bathe before he came to her.

His sharp intake of breath and then a low curse, though she could not imagine what might have happened. She had been tempted to call out to him to see if all was well, but she did not. Instead she had remained still and silent in the bed, waiting for him.

As she waited for him now…waiting and wondering if perhaps he had fallen asleep at the table. It had been such a long ride that he must be exhausted—

"Are you still awake, wife?"

Nora blinked in surprise at Niall's imposing silhouette in the doorway, his powerful body limned in firelight from the hearth.

A powerful body, she realized with a start, that was completely bared to her gaze, and she sharply drew in her breath.

"Y-yes." Her voice no more than a squeak, Nora felt as if her face was afire as he moved toward the bed with athletic strides. She thought her heart might leap out of her chest when he flipped aside the blanket and climbed into the bed beside her, the mattress depressing beneath his weight.

She was naked. He was naked. Oh God…

"Breathe, Nora."

Breathe? She heard his low chuckle, but could no more take a full breath than she could calm her racing heartbeat. Only when he rolled onto his side and propped himself on his elbow to look down at her, did she gasp in surprise.

His beard was gone! He smiled at her amazement, a slow lazy smile that stilled her breath anew and sent a flush of warmth to her toes. Truly, she had never seen a man more handsome than Niall O'Byrne.

And never before had she felt so lacking to be lying next to such a man…married to such a man. She swallowed hard, blinking back tears.

Foolish tears that made her feel even worse and more wretchedly sorry for Niall that she hadn't been born a stunning beauty like her sister Kristina, who would have been a far more fitting match—

"More tears, Nora? Here I had thought my shaving might please you. I even cut myself—"

"You cut yourself?"

He nodded and she saw it then, the nick at his jawline that still oozed a fine streak of blood. That must have been why he'd cursed earlier! Forgetting her distress, Nora sat bolt upright in the bed.

"Oh, Niall, is there anything I can do? Shall I fetch a

cloth for you? It's still bleeding!"

"Easy, wife. I'll not expire from a shaving cut…though perhaps I might from looking upon you."

His voice had grown so husky, Nora could only stare at him blankly…until she realized his gaze had strayed to her breasts.

Her breasts that were fully bared to him when she'd sat up, the blanket pooled at her waist. Her cheeks firing, she sought at once to lift the blanket but he stayed her hand, slowly shaking his head.

"No, woman. I want to see you."

Niall found that it was suddenly difficult for him to speak, his throat having grown tight at the perfectly rounded breasts mere inches from his mouth.

At the hardened nipples so taut and rosy as if beckoning to him.

Aye, he had seen her naked earlier at the church…but that was before she had become his bride. He had seen the flawless beauty of her figure beneath a soaked sleeping gown clinging to her bare skin…and so had the priest, who had immediately turned away while Niall had focused upon the urgent task at hand.

Now he focused as well upon the new task at hand…one that rested with him to make as pleasurable for her as possible.

Oddly enough, he felt somewhat like an untried youth, much to his chagrin. He was well versed in satisfying a woman, but he had abstained from any dalliances once he had become betrothed to Caitlin. As their wedding day had grown closer his hunger to possess her had reached a fever pitch, only to be doused as if with ice-cold water once she had chosen another man over him.

To soothe his torment, he could have bedded any number of women at the tavern in Ostmentown, but drinking heavily had proved his only solace. Now Niall felt his hands trembling, it had been so long since he had known a woman…and this wasn't just any woman.

Damn it all, he would think no more of Caitlin MacMurrough this night but direct all of his attention upon his new bride!

"Lie down, Nora." Again Niall found it hard to speak, as a part of him too long restrained grew hard and thick beneath the blanket. Seeing to his own needs for over two agonizing years had been no substitute for the heated softness of a woman's body, but he knew he must take care to move slowly. "I want to look at all of you."

Still propped upon one elbow, he could see that she trembled as she nodded, which did not surprise him. With a ragged sigh, she lay back down while he flipped the blanket to the foot of the bed. At once her hands flew to cover her nakedness, her fingers splayed above the dusky triangle at the heart of her thighs.

Slender thighs and long shapely legs that made Niall's throat grow tighter.

She was neither tall nor short but somewhere in between, her body perfectly proportioned. He ached suddenly to touch her, to caress the tempting curve of her narrow waist and the ripe fullness of her hips, but somehow restrained himself.

Not yet. Instead he caught her hands in his and drew them to his lips, and began to tenderly kiss her long, slender fingers. He felt her shivering suddenly as if cold, her pale pink areolas puckering, and her creamy flesh dimpling with goosebumps, which told him much.

His innocent bride had never been kissed before. Never been touched by a man before. He could not deny that the realization pleased him, and without wasting another moment he lowered his head and pressed his mouth to hers.

She started, her body going rigid beneath him, but only for an instant as he kissed her soft lips until he felt her start to relax.

He kissed her still as he heard her sigh against his mouth, her breath warm and sweet and melding with his own. Unbidden thoughts of the last woman he'd kissed assailed him again, but he did his best to force Caitlin from his mind.

Nora was his bride. Nora was the *only* woman that mattered to him now, Niall told himself fiercely. She was his to protect, to cherish as well as he would allow himself to, and to make love to as should any husband and wife.

Aye, and he wanted to make love to her. Already his breathing had grown faster, harder, his shaft swelling almost painfully. Yet once again he reminded himself to move slowly and awaken her gently to the ways of man and woman—God grant him patience!

He lifted his mouth from hers to find her eyes closed

and her body gone limp against him, although her lovely breasts rose and fell in a manner that also told him much.

His kiss had moved her. His touch had stirred her. He found himself smiling that mere kissing could arouse her so. Such a response bespoke a deep passion inside her just waiting to be unleashed.

"Did you enjoy that, wife?"

CHAPTER 6

Nora fluttered open her eyes to find Niall smiling down at her, that same lazy smile that made her heart beat faster.

Had she enjoyed his kiss? All she could muster was a soft "Aye," she felt so breathless and lightheaded, Nora certain she could never have imagined anything so wondrous.

"Would you like some more?"

His smile had broadened as if her reply had pleased him, and she smiled too, at his husky teasing. "Aye, husband—"

The words were no sooner said than he'd found her mouth again, his kiss so achingly tender that she moaned against his lips. She'd never made such a sound before but could not help herself…and she heard herself moan again when the pressure of his mouth suddenly grew harder, more insistent.

Instinctively she parted her lips beneath his and he swept his tongue into her mouth, something so raw igniting within her that she felt shaken to her toes. She seemed to know innately what to do, her tongue swirling with his, and this time it was Niall who groaned against her mouth.

"Woman…"

Oh no, had she displeased him? Feeling a sudden sense of panic, Nora drew back from him to find Niall searching her face in the firelight emanating from the door left ajar. It seemed his eyes locked with hers, something wordless passing between them, and he shook his head as if fighting with himself.

"Nora, it is your first time. I don't want to rush you. Hurt you."

She knew nothing of the passion shared between a man and a woman, but Nora realized then that she hadn't displeased Niall at all.

He had groaned against her mouth because he wanted her. Desired her.

And she desired him. So deeply, so wildly that she reached up to caress his face, her fingers trembling even as she felt his body trembling against her. He seemed to shudder at her touch, and took her hand in his larger one to press a heated kiss into her palm that took her breath away.

Yet it was his mouth suddenly at her breast that made her cry out. Something animal seemed to explode in him as he drew her nipple between his teeth and slid his fingers into the slippery wetness between her thighs.

As he lightly nipped her and then suckled hungrily, it seemed she had lost all power over her body. Unconsciously she parted her thighs to him, allowing his fingers to slide even more deeply inside her even as she arched against his hand.

Something animal exploded in her, too, as she reached up to clutch his shoulders while he covered her with his body, his heavily muscled weight pressing her deep into the mattress.

She felt him spread her legs wide with his knee, his breathing hard, her breathing ragged, his splayed fingers cupping her bottom as he thrust himself into her so fiercely that she screamed.

Not from the sudden pain, searing for only an instant, but from the blinding intensity of sensations rocking her and stealing her breath.

She could only fling her arms around his neck and cling to him as he thrust into her again and again, his powerful body shaking and bathed in sweat. She shook, too, uncontrollably now, until she heard herself scream again at the sensation of his hot seed exploding inside her, his body throbbing violently.

She could but arch her hips against his as her own climax seized her, lifting her up, up into dazzling light that burst before her tightly closed eyes.

She could not say how long she hung suspended in such incredible bliss...until suddenly she felt as if she were spinning and tumbling as Niall rolled with her onto his back.

When at last she opened her eyes long moments later, she lay atop him, her tangled hair covering her face, his arms holding her tightly.

She could not have been more astonished when she heard his low rumble of laughter, one of his hands sliding down her back to give her bottom a gentle squeeze.

"So much for not rushing you, wife."

He began to laugh harder and she could not help giggling, too, even as exhaustion overwhelmed her and she felt unable to keep her eyes open any longer.

The last thing she heard as sleep overcame her was Niall's husky voice as he once more wrapped his arms tightly around her.

"Aye, rest now, Nora O'Byrne. Rest."

Her eyes still closed, Nora yawned and stretched her arms way above her head as she rolled to one side—and then gasped as a strong masculine arm grabbed her right before she tumbled from the bed. The next thing she knew she was gathered close against Niall, who lay on his side next to her…smiling.

She blinked at him in the sunlight filtering into the room from tiny cracks in the timbered walls, wondering how this man could make her heartbeat suddenly race so wildly.

And not just any man…but her *husband*. Her face grew hot as impassioned memories of their lovemaking came rushing back to her. Aye, she was truly his wife now, wedded and bedded—oh God.

Niall's smile had grown broader, and she sensed that he knew exactly what she'd just been thinking, which only made her cheeks burn hotter. Yet the good humor dancing in his blue-gray eyes made her smile at him, too, although with some embarrassment.

"A good morning to you, Nora O'Byrne. Did you sleep soundly?"

Nora O'Byrne. She couldn't deny her new name had a fine ring to it, and she nodded, liking very much to hear Niall saying it, too.

"Aye, I did. And you?"

He sobered suddenly, and shrugged his shoulders, though she could see the teasing in his eyes. "Well, other than a wee bit of snoring from my new bride—"

"Snoring?" Nora's hand flew to her mouth, uncertain of whether he'd spoken the truth or not. She must have looked horrified, because Niall at once gathered her closer to him as he chuckled.

"No, wife, you barely made a peep…and there's no wonder why. You and I made a fine pair in our impatience to seal our wedding vows."

His voice filled with a now familiar huskiness that made her shiver, Nora felt her breath still as he bent his head to kiss her forehead.

The tip of her nose.

And then her lips, his mouth so warm…so wonderfully warm. Yet he had no more kissed her when he drew back again to look into her eyes. He'd sobered again, but this time his gaze held no humor.

"I'd like nothing more than to stay abed with you, but we must go. It's well past dawn and we've another few hours' journey ahead of us before we're home."

Home.

Niall's home in Glenmalure, and soon to be hers as well. Aye, she knew they must leave this place, but as Niall threw aside the blanket and rose from the bed she felt a tinge of sadness.

Their wedding night was done. Already he strode toward the door, his naked body so magnificent that she could not tear her gaze away from him…the broadness of his back, his taut buttocks and long, muscular legs. Yet he suddenly turned around and came back to the bed, affording her a clear view of that impressive part of him that last night had thrust so powerfully into the very heart of her.

Her face burning, she felt that she couldn't breathe. Had he changed his mind and they would linger here for a while longer? She shifted upon the mattress to make more room for him to join her, but instead he stopped at the side of the bed and held out his hand to her.

"Up with you, wife. We've a fine big bed awaiting us in Glenmalure where we'll have nights aplenty to share together. Will you rise and dress swiftly now so we can be on our way?"

She bobbed her head and took his hand, astounded again at the miracle her life had become as Niall pulled her up from the bed.

"What do you mean my bride is gone?" His outraged

roar echoing from the rafters of the great hall, Sigurd Knutson swept the faces in front of him from a pale Magnus MacTorkil and his wide-eyed wife Agnes, to a cluster of servants nervously wringing their hands.

No answer came but a collective shaking of heads and worried glances, which only made Sigurd more incensed.

He wanted to kill something! To plunge his axe into something! If there was no bride, there would be no wedding this day and by Odin, he hadn't sailed all the way from Norway to Éire for his own amusement! Spying a young dog lying underneath a nearby table, Sigurd strode over furiously and gave the animal a swift kick, its pained yelps making everyone around him jump.

"Have you searched the stronghold?" he bellowed, wheeling to face them again.

"Aye, Lord Knutson, and we're still searching," Magnus replied tightly, the stout, gray-bearded merchant clearly not appreciating such a display of foul temper.

Yet what did Sigurd care? These Ostmen needed him far more than he needed them, though the gold he'd been promised if he wed Nora MacTorkil had admittedly made him sail all the faster to Éire. He ground his teeth. If no bride, then no gold—by all the gods in Valhalla! His fury was so great he was certain his blood had begun to boil.

"Agnes, you saw her last, did you not?" Turning his wrath upon his beanpole of a cousin, Sigurd strode forward to tower above her, the woman's pinched face gone white.

"Aye, Sigurd, my maidservants and I put her to bed— and I left them to sit outside her door—"

"They saw nothing? Heard nothing?"

"Not a peep! She must have slipped out the window during the night…but as my husband said, we're looking for her everywhere. There is no way she could have left the stronghold so she must be hiding—"

"Hiding from *me*? Sigurd Skullcrusher? A lord of the house of Earl Hakon, my own cousin, who one day will be king of all Norway? She's fortunate that I would even look in her direction, the plain-faced chit! Did you teach her no obedience?"

Sigurd was so incensed now that he'd spewed spittle in all directions, Agnes wiping a thin sticky strand from her cheek.

"She's never done anything like this before, Sigurd! It must have been nervousness over the wedding, I'm certain of it! All is prepared, the marriage feast and Father Gilbert here to perform the ceremony. We will find her, I promise you. *We* promise you, aye, Magnus?"

"Aye," came the Ostman's terse answer, while Sigurd began furiously to pace in front of them.

"You say you're searching everywhere, MacTorkil, but is there any chance she might have fled from the stronghold?" he demanded.

"No chance at all, the guards at the main gate saw nothing. No one left or entered last night but a driver and his wagon to fetch more ale—"

"Damn the bastards, I'll skewer their corpses to the gate myself!" Sigurd was already striding to the doors of the great hall, the dozen strapping Norsemen who'd accompanied him falling in behind him. "My bride is cleverer than you gave her credit for, MacTorkil! When I find her, a good beating will come before the wedding, and *that* I promise! She'll learn not to defy her elders or her husband ever again!"

CHAPTER 7

Nora wrapped her arms more tightly around Niall and breathed in the sweet summer air scented with wildflowers.

She'd never seen a place like Glenmalure. The steep-sided valley flanked by rugged mountains lay awash in light and shadow as the midday sun peeked behind puffy white clouds and then disappeared again. Niall had told her that his brother Ronan's stronghold lay at the other end so they still had a bit of a ride ahead of them, but that would give her some time to calm her emotions.

Aye, she was nervous to meet his family and excited, too, she couldn't deny it.

Her new family. The infamous O'Byrnes that were known throughout Éire as a fierce rebel clan whose lands no men trespassed upon if they valued their lives.

She'd heard many a tale in her father's great hall of Ronan O'Byrne and his men's countless raids against the Normans, the Ostmen envious of their brash daring and dreaming of such exploits themselves. Niall's elder brother had been described as the very devil himself, with midnight black hair and slate gray eyes that darkened when angered, and black clothing when raiding that had earned him the ominous name Black O'Byrne.

Would Ronan be pleased to see Niall again? Niall had told her only that he'd been away for two months and that he and his brother hadn't parted well, his face grown so serious that she hadn't pressed him to tell her why. Yet when Niall had mentioned Ronan's wife Triona, once an O'Toole, another famed rebel clan, his expression had gone from dark to light in an instant and he'd burst out laughing.

Nora had realized then how fond Niall was of his fiery-haired sister-in-law. During the ride when he'd shared with her the tale of Ronan and Triona's tempestuous courtship, Nora felt truly eager to meet this unconventional young woman who had won the heart of Ronan Black O'Byrne.

Yet it was when Niall had mentioned his younger sister Maire that Nora had sensed not only his love for her, but deep unspoken concern. Once again Niall had said little else and Nora had grown quiet with him, just hugging him close and knowing that soon she would learn much about her new home and family. So they had ridden for the past half hour in companionable silence, but now she felt Niall growing tense as he kicked their mount into a canter.

"Are you ready to start an uproar?" he shouted above the gelding's pounding hooves as they rode down a rocky slope, Nora's hair flying behind her.

She squeezed him tight and nodded against his broad shoulder.

In truth she had no idea what Niall meant, but she knew as certain as she was eternally grateful for the new life he'd given her that she'd find out very soon.

Ronan sat at the far end of the feasting-hall, staring into the fire burning in the immense hearth. Thankfully the place was empty but for servants clearing away the remnants of the midday meal, his clansmen, their wives, and their children gone about their daily affairs.

So, too, had Triona left him to put their little Deirdre to bed for her afternoon nap, well, if she could get their willful fourteen-month-old daughter to agree to lie down. Born as stubborn as her mother, Deirdre preferred to play with her toys or totter after her snow-white kitten until she crumpled with exhaustion, and only then would Triona be able to scoop her up and deposit her in her bed.

Aye, it was a daily tug-of-war between his beautiful wife and daughter, which made Ronan smile to himself though he quickly sobered. Deirdre possessed her mother's headstrong temperament and unruly curls, midnight black instead of coppery red, but her soft gray eyes reminded him so much of his sister Maire.

By God, why did the pain of her leaving Glenmalure with Lord Duncan FitzWilliam still cut him so deeply? No doubt they were married now, his sweet lovely sister wed to one of the most powerful Norman barons in the land.

Irish and Norman! It seemed the world Ronan knew was changing around him every day. Though reared from infancy as an O'Toole, Triona bore Norman blood in her veins and MacMurrough, too, that clan loyal to England's King John a hated enemy of the O'Byrnes not so long ago.

His daughter Deirdre bore Norman blood, and any children born to Maire and Duncan would be the same. Yet Ronan fully intended to continue his raids against the vile intruders that forty years' past had begun their scourge upon Éire, stealing land, raping, and murdering.

Ronan's fist tightened around his ale cup, and he lowered his head with a heavy sigh.

Mayhap that was why his pain ran so deep. He felt torn, and he knew it.

Duncan FitzWilliam had shown himself to be an honorable man unlike any Norman that Ronan had ever encountered. Triona had tried to convince him as much, and Niall as well before he'd disappeared to God-knows-where, but enraged at both of them Ronan had refused to listen.

It was only when Duncan had ridden courageously into Glenmalure—*alone!*—to fetch his bride four days ago that Ronan had seen for himself the true mettle of the man.

A Norman! How it galled Ronan still, but he wanted Maire to be happy so he had forgiven her as best he could.

He had suspended raids for a time, again, for Maire's sake, but he knew it would not be forever. If Ronan bent too far against everything he believed in, everything he'd fought for, he would break—

"Ronan!"

The bellowing voice of his clansman Flann O'Faelin

echoed in the feasting-hall. Ronan rose at once from the table, thinking something must be amiss. From the look on the giant carrot-haired Irishman's face as he rushed toward Ronan, he was certain of it.

"Flann?"

"A rider comes across the glen, Ronan—and by all the saints, I believe it's Niall!"

Ronan had already rushed past his clansman before Flann had finished uttering the words. He could hear already a great commotion outside the feasting-hall, excited shouts and whistles, and he knew everyone must be rushing to the inner palisade of stout red oak.

Only days ago they had thought it was Niall returned home at last, but it had been Duncan FitzWilliam instead. As Ronan ran outside into the sunlight, it seemed all faces were turned expectantly toward him for the signal only he or Niall could give to open the three massive sets of gates that guarded the stronghold.

A signal he gave at once, Ronan trusting implicitly Flann's pronouncement that the rider must be Niall.

Intense relief filled Ronan, as well as a blaze of anger.

Where the devil had Niall been these past two months? His long absence had fueled many sleepless nights and endless anxiety for himself, Triona, and his clansmen, who now began to cheer wildly.

Aye, his younger brother and own Tanist was nothing if not loved by all who knew him. Again Ronan felt immense relief as he made his way through the crush of his people as the first set of gates, the tallest and heaviest, was hauled open by the eight strong men needed for the task.

"Ronan, is it true?"

He spun to meet Triona, her lovely face alight and her coppery curls flying as she ran toward him and threw herself into his arms. "Niall's come home?"

Ronan hugged her tightly, nodding. Together they hastened through the outer two sets of gates built into the massive earthen ramparts while their clansmen whooped and waved to the approaching rider.

Thankfulness overwhelming him, Ronan watched as Niall raised his arm in greeting and reined in his lathered mount in front of them.

Remorse flooded Ronan, too. The last time he'd seen Niall he had struck his brother for claiming that Duncan FitzWilliam must be an honorable man for Maire to have fallen in love with him. Ronan saw at once that Niall must be recalling that wretched moment as well from the wary look on his face.

Yet it wasn't his guarded expression so much that drew Ronan's attention but that Niall wasn't alone.

A young, auburn-haired woman held him fast around the waist and stared wide-eyed over his shoulder at all the commotion as cheering O'Byrnes surrounded them.

Ronan saw that Triona stared too, open-mouthed, as she glanced from him to Niall, whose one hand held the reins while his free hand gripped the woman's arms as if to reassure her.

Ronan doubted he had ever seen his beloved wife look so surprised, or struck virtually speechless. And was that a priest's robe the woman was wearing?

"Ronan, Triona, my clansmen!" came Niall's raised voice above the din, everyone falling silent around him. "It's been a long ride for us so I pray you offer a fine welcome to my bride, Nora O'Byrne!"

Bride? As Ronan's own mouth dropped open, he doubted if Niall had suddenly sprouted two heads, his people would have looked more astonished.

Everyone merely stared, silent, while Niall's mount nickered and bobbed his head as if confirming what Niall had just announced.

Only Triona quickly regained her composure and left Ronan's side to rush forward, her arms outstretched to Niall as he dismounted to embrace her tightly. "Oh, Niall, I'm so glad you're home!" Yet she'd no sooner disengaged herself, glancing over her shoulder pointedly at Ronan, when she reached up to squeeze the young woman's hand. "Welcome to Glenmalure, Nora!"

"Aye, shall we stand here all day outside the gates?" Ronan shouted, his mind overrun by questions as Niall shot him a glance that still held wariness. "We've casks of wine to tap and a marriage feast to prepare! Niall is safe and *finally* home among us again…and with a new wife! Tonight we'll celebrate!"

Nora leaned her head back against the tub, her head still spinning from how quickly she'd gone from atop a horse to a warm, soaking bath that felt like heaven.

Aye, Niall had been right! Their arrival had started an uproar unlike anything she'd seen in her life. Riding across the glen had been exhilarating enough, but when they had stopped in front of the imposing gates as people spilled out from the stronghold, Nora doubted she had ever felt her heart beating so wildly.

The cheering and the shouting had been deafening…only to subside into stunned silence and thunderstruck stares as soon as Niall had announced to his clansmen that he'd brought home a bride. Why had they gaped so? Had Niall sworn never to marry or some such thing?

Thank God the beautiful young woman Nora had recognized from Niall's vivid description as Triona had rushed through the crowd to warmly greet them. Meanwhile Ronan Black O'Byrne, his expression inscrutable, had taken charge and sent everyone hastening back into the stronghold.

Standing taller than most men and with his midnight hair, Nora had known at once that the formidable-looking rebel as handsome as his wife was lovely was Niall's older brother and chieftain of the Glenmalure O'Byrnes.

Nora had sensed, too, the palpable tension between the two men, which both puzzled and concerned her. Yet thankfully they had locked arms to greet each other when she, Niall, and their exhausted horse were swept into the stronghold by the boisterous O'Byrnes who had begun to cheer again.

The next thing Nora knew, Niall had lifted her to the

ground in front of a dwelling-house he had murmured in her ear was their home. She didn't have a chance to utter a word, though, when he immediately handed her off to Triona and strode away with Ronan.

Nora had stared after him, stunned, her heart sinking.

She imagined Niall and his brother had much to discuss, but to leave her without a kiss or embrace? What of the intimacy they had shared only hours ago? Aye, she knew well enough that he hadn't married her out of love, but did he have no tender regard for her at all?

A gentle squeeze at her elbow had broken into her thoughts, and Nora had met Triona's stunning emerald eyes to find she looked troubled. Why that would be Nora had no clue, but there had been no time to dwell upon it as Triona led her inside the dwelling-house.

At once the place had come alive with maidservants bearing buckets of hot water, wine, and food. It seemed that before Nora could blink she had been gently stripped of her clothing and settled into a tub set by the hearth that surely was large enough for Niall, which had made her heart race. She missed him so, she couldn't deny it. Nor that her feelings for him like a yearning ache seemed only to be growing—

"How is the water? Warm enough?"

Startled from her thoughts, Nora nodded at Triona, who gestured for a maidservant to stack several linen towels atop a stool set within her reach. "Aye, it's wonderful," she murmured as another girl poured a stream of lavender-scented oil into the tub. "Thank you, Triona—

may I call you Triona?"

"Of course you can, we're sisters now!" Triona flashed Nora a warm smile and then glanced over her shoulder at an oaken table surrounded by heavy carved chairs. "There's a bowl of venison stew and wine for you when you've finished bathing…and a choice of gowns laid out upon the bed in the next room. They're some of my own, mayhap a wee bit short for you, but I'm sure they'll fit well enough. I'll set the seamstresses to sewing you some new ones straightaway."

Triona gave a light laugh. "If Niall has told you anything about me, you'll know that I once hated gowns and refused to wear the useless things, but I've grown used to them now. And Ronan likes them…"

The softness in Triona's voice when she'd spoken her husband's name made Nora smile, too, though she suddenly felt so wistful. "Aye, Niall has shared some stories…but we haven't known each other very long…not even a day—"

"Jesu, Mary, and Joseph, no wonder."

Triona had spoken almost to herself, but her gaze held such compassion now that Nora felt that something must surely be amiss.

"Triona?"

She got no answer. Triona had already spun on her heel and hastened from the dwelling-house, leaving Nora to stare after her in surprise.

CHAPTER 8

"Niall O'Byrne!"

His back to the entrance of the feasting-hall, Niall shook his head at the outraged sound of Triona's voice.

He'd suspected this moment would come, and he glanced at Ronan, who merely shrugged his broad shoulders. All around them the preparations for the wedding feast continued unabated as if no one had heard Triona's outburst, everyone well used to lively discussions held by Ronan, Triona, and Niall near the huge hearth.

"She doesn't look happy, brother," Ronan said, rising from the table where he and Niall had been sitting to greet his wife, and Niall knew then she was almost upon them. He rose, too, and turned to face Triona as she stormed right up to him, her vivid green eyes flashing fire.

"Niall O'Byrne, how could you? Marry a girl you've known for no more than a day? A girl you don't love?"

"Easy, Triona, if you'd let me explain—"

"*Explain*? Aye, you'd better tell me quick enough how this has come about—and with the poor girl already pining for you while you've no like feelings for her at all! I saw it from the first when you left her without a gentle word or even a kiss on the cheek, but I was hoping and praying it wasn't so—"

"Pining?" Niall stared in confusion at Triona, who stared back at him with her hands fisted at her hips as if she couldn't believe what he'd just said.

"Aye, pining! Have you gone daft, Niall? I love you dearly and I'm overjoyed you're home, but I could kick you right now! No more than a day and yet you've already bedded her?"

"Aye, Triona, but if you'll only listen—"

"Begorra, Niall, I never thought you for a fool but if you've bedded her, no wonder she bears feelings for you! She's opened her heart to you now while you act as if she's no one special to you at all—"

"Triona, let Niall speak!"

Ronan's roar more of exasperation than anger, Niall felt a sweeping sense of relief as Triona clapped her mouth shut though she still stared at him indignantly.

In truth he felt jolted by what she'd revealed to him about Nora because he hadn't realized she might have begun to care for him…or else he simply hadn't wanted to think about it. Damn it all, why had things suddenly grown so complicated?

"Ronan has heard everything I had to tell, Triona, but I'll repeat it for you as well. I saved Nora from drowning last night—"

"Oh, aye, so that's why you took her to wife?"

Very much aware that all commotion in the feasting-hall had ceased, everyone now rooted where they stood to listen, Niall shrugged his shoulders and rushed on. He had nothing to hide from his clansmen or from Triona, either.

He could see at once that she began to relax in his telling of how he'd dragged Nora from the River Liffey and carried her to the nearby church and the old priest there, and how Nora's stark terror had so moved him to marry her. One glance around the feasting-hall told him that everyone appeared riveted by his tale and he kept going with their escape from Ostmentown and the long ride home.

He didn't go into detail about their one stop for the night, and thankfully Triona didn't press him. Instead she had sunk onto a bench, where she simply shook her head.

"Ostmentown, Niall? That's where you've been these past two months when we didn't know if you were alive or dead?"

"Aye, drinking and sleeping it off on the dock…until Nora tripped over me and tumbled into the river. When I jumped in after her, *that* sobered me up well enough."

Niall was grateful that Triona didn't press him, either, about why he'd spent so much time in a drunken stupor. She knew full well that Caitlin and her betrayal lay at the heart of it.

"So now we've the daughter of the renowned merchant Magnus MacTorkil among us…and Nora a promised bride to another man," Ronan interjected grimly, which made Niall bristle.

"What was I to do? Leave her at the church where this Sigurd Knutson she claimed a monster might find her? The priest swore to me he'd tell no one what transpired there—"

"*If* his word is to be trusted."

"A *priest*, Ronan," Niall said with growing exasperation. "If you cannot trust such a man…" He didn't say more, unease suddenly growing in the pit of his stomach that Father Edmund might betray them.

"Couldn't you have simply brought her here without marrying her first?" Triona said, cutting into the discussion that seemed to be growing tenser by the moment. "We would have offered her protection—"

"Enough, the thing is done!" Niall's incensed roar echoed from the rafters, while everyone in the feasting-hall quickly went back to their tasks. "I waited for two years for Caitlin MacMurrough to become my bride! What difference if I took another in less than two hours? Nora is my wife with all that entails—"

"But you don't love her, Niall!" Triona interjected, rushing over to him to grasp his arm. "Aye, it was a heroic thing you did…but a terrible one, too. For Nora, for you. I fear it's still Caitlin that you love—"

"Damn it all, there shall be no feast!" Enraged now, Niall could not bear remaining in the hall another moment.

He could not bear Ronan staring at him grimly while tears glistened in Triona's eyes, his brave, outspoken sister-in-law who rarely cried.

He could not bear his clansmen watching him uncomfortably, everyone rooted in place again as a strained silence filled the vast room.

Uttering a vehement curse, Niall grabbed the first thing he saw, an open cask of wine. Never before Caitlin's treachery had he been a man to drown himself in drink, but now he couldn't think of anything better to ease the fury boiling inside him.

The gut-wrenching pain that had come roaring back to devour him.

Hoisting the cask to his shoulder, Niall stormed toward the doors and shut his mind and his heart to Ronan and Triona calling after him.

"So the woman Niall was to marry is named Caitlin?"

Triona nodded at Nora's soft query and squeezed her hand, making Nora feel as if her world had grown so dark again.

So terribly dark. Sitting together at the table where Nora had just finished eating venison stew, she felt, too, that she might be sick.

Triona had come to tell her that there would be no marriage feast, and that Nora should not expect Niall to return to their dwelling-house that night, either.

There had been a disagreement and angry words…and Niall had stormed from the feasting-hall with a cask of wine and taken himself off somewhere in the stronghold.

Nora swallowed hard and glanced down at the exquisite blue silk gown she wore, so like the costly ones she had known in Ostmentown.

She had prepared so eagerly for the celebration of her and Niall's marriage from her freshly washed hair brushed to a glossy sheen to the borrowed finery she wore and the soft leather slippers upon her feet. She had even opened the soiled leather pouch she had found in the saddlebag brought into the dwelling-house by a maidservant, and dumped the glittering contents upon the bed. Meanwhile the fresh-faced girl at once had whisked away Nora's still damp sleeping gown and cloak to be cleaned and hung out to dry.

Nora's hands had trembled as she adorned herself with delicate gold arm-rings and a priceless jeweled brooch at her shoulder, gifts from her parents in happier days. Yet the one thing she had wanted to wear, a gold filigree ring set with a brilliant blue sapphire that had once belonged to her sister Kristina, was missing.

Had it slipped from the pouch when she'd fallen into the river? Now Nora toyed distractedly with her bare index finger as Triona stared at her silently, her lovely green eyes once again filled with compassion.

"I should have come sooner to let you know about the feast," Triona said gently, shaking her head. "I had hoped Niall might think better of his anger and change his mind, but he didn't return. Aye, you deserved as well to know how Niall came to be in Ostmentown—"

"She's very beautiful, isn't she? Caitlin?"

Triona didn't answer readily, but then sighed. "Aye, but her beauty hid a fickle heart, though we did not see it. Not in time to save Niall from such misery—"

"Ah, God!" Feeling so stricken by the tale Triona had shared with her of how Niall had waited so long to marry the woman he loved, only to have her choose another, Nora lunged from the chair.

Scalding tears filled her eyes, but she would not weep. She refused to weep! Instead she began to pace around the room, hugging her arms to her chest.

How could her marriage to Niall ever surmount the love he'd felt for Caitlin...or the terrible anguish he'd suffered at her betrayal? The anguish he still suffered!

"Nora..."

She barely heard Triona utter her name, but hugged herself more tightly. If she did not keep pacing, Nora was certain she would double over and crumple to the floor.

What was she to do? No doubt he loved Caitlin still! Niall's pain was proof of that...while here she had entertained such romantic notions that her new life with him was a miracle.

Ridiculous notions! Mayhap he now thought his decision to wed her a curse!

"Nora, please stop!"

Triona blocked her path and drew her into her arms to hug her, while Nora could only drop her head to Triona's shoulder and quietly weep.

"He saved my life...and married me to protect me..."

"Aye, so he did. Niall has always been good-hearted and the most caring of men. He helped me find my way to Ronan...and Maire to Duncan FitzWilliam—"

"But there's no hope for happiness! How can there

be?"

"Jesu, Mary, and Joseph, there's always hope!" Her voice grown stern, Triona drew back from Nora to stare into her eyes. "Enough with this foolishness, Nora O'Byrne! You know the truth now and you must do your best to overcome it! Aye, sobbing might soothe you for a bit, but it will do nothing to bring you and Niall closer together."

Triona left her and went to the table to fetch a linen cloth, and then hastened back to dab away the tears herself from Nora's flushed cheeks.

"There now. You look lovely as can be in that blue gown and you've the prettiest eyes I've ever seen…but best they not be red from crying, are we agreed?"

Nora nodded, and gasped in surprise when Triona took her arm and rushed with her toward the door.

"You're Niall's wife now so you must go to him! Share his pain and do your best to make him smile again."

"But where? I don't know the stronghold—"

"I've a good idea where he might be and it's not too far away. I saw the door ajar to Maire's dwelling-house so he must be grieving, too, that he didn't have a chance to tell her goodbye. She left Glenmalure only four days past with Lord FitzWilliam although we don't talk much about that here. It still vexes Ronan greatly that she's gone to wed a Norman."

With that, Triona pulled Nora outside into the waning afternoon sunshine and together they hurried to an adjacent stout wooden structure almost identical to Niall's.

Nora's head still spun from everything Triona had told her, but her breath stilled altogether when Triona pushed her inside and shut the door soundly behind her.

For a moment Nora heard nothing but her heartbeat thundering in her ears…until she heard boots scraping upon the floor and the distinct sound of wine being poured into a cup. The dwelling-house was so dark, the windows shuttered, a single guttering candle the only light in the main room.

"Niall?"

CHAPTER 9

"Go away!"

At the fierceness in his voice, Nora almost heeded him and fled.

You're Niall's wife now so you must go to him! Share his pain and do your best to make him smile again.

Somehow Triona's impassioned words echoing in her mind made Nora stand her ground, though she trembled.

"Niall, it's me. Nora. May—may I speak to you?"

She heard nothing but silence in response, which made her heart sink.

Of course he wouldn't wish to speak to her! She wasn't at all the woman of his dreams...but the wife that dire circumstances had foisted upon him—

"Come forward if you wish, woman, but you won't like what you see."

Nora swallowed hard and once more fought the urge to turn and run.

Now wasn't the right time. She could tell from his slurred speech that he'd downed more than his share of wine, so how could anything she said make sense to him?

"Aye, she's fled...a good thing," she heard him mutter, which made Nora lift her chin and venture a few steps forward.

"No, I'm here."

"Ah, then come and join me, wife, and I'll pour you some wine!"

Nora gasped as Niall seemed to materialize out of the shadows to take her hand and pull her with him deeper into the room. The next thing she knew he had pushed her none-too-gently into a chair within the golden circle of light cast by the solitary candle.

He stood so tall above her, swaying slightly, and raised his cup to her before taking a long, deep swallow.

God help her, he was worse off than she had feared...this man who had only been kind to her and saved her from a fate that would have surely meant her death. That thought alone flooded her with pity, her heart going out to him.

"Niall...I'm so sorry about Caitlin. It must have been so terrible for you...is still so terrible—"

"By God, who told you about Caitlin?"

His roar had made her jump, but when he turned suddenly and hurled the cup against the opposite wall, Nora lunged from the chair to run to the door. She knew he came after her, and she cried out when he caught her by the waist to spin her around to face him.

"Triona told me! She thought I should know what you've suffered—oh Niall, you're frightening me!"

At once his hands fell from her waist and he stood there, no longer swaying, his features inscrutable in the dark. She heard him sigh, though, a deep shuddering sigh that sounded like a groan as he turned and left her standing by herself at the door.

Her eyes growing accustomed to the dim light, she saw him slump into a chair and lean forward to hold his head in his hands.

"God help me, Nora, forgive me."

His voice sounded so bleak that she could but rush toward him, her heart aching for him anew. She dropped to her knees beside his chair and flung her arms around him, and rested her head upon his shoulder.

"Oh Niall, you've no cause to ask my forgiveness! You've suffered so—"

"And you haven't suffered as well?" His voice ragged, Niall lifted his head to stare at her, his gaze tormented in the candlelight. "To have wished for the river to claim you rather than face the man...no, the monster as you called him that your family had ordained that you must wed? I told you I would never hurt you...and yet what did I do just now?"

"Only frightened me a little..."

"A little?" Niall gave a short laugh, but it held no humor. He dropped his head into his hands again and exhaled heavily as if in despair, while Nora rested her hand upon his forearm, not knowing what else she might say to soothe him.

She glanced around her then, for the first time noticing

the room's feminine trappings in the flickering light. She had seen nothing finer even in the luxurious rooms of her father's house…hangings of painted cloth upon the walls, a richly colored woven carpet that cushioned her knees, and delicately wrought candleholders made of gold.

Nora noticed suddenly, too, the fragrant scent of wild roses, a fresh bouquet of pink blossoms in a vase set atop a white-clothed table as if the occupant might return at any moment to enjoy them. Yet Triona had told her that Maire had left Glenmalure with her Norman lord only days ago, and that Niall hadn't been there to tell her goodbye…

"Niall, tell me about Maire."

Nora had spoken barely above a whisper, but at once she felt Niall's arm grow tense and she wondered if she'd made his suffering worse.

"Only if you wish to," she added quickly, yet she gasped when Niall suddenly reached around to lift her into his lap and settle her against him. She was so astonished that she could only gape at him. Niall held her so close that his warm breath, scented with wine, fanned her cheek.

"I'll tell you about Maire if you tell me of your life in Ostmentown. You've heard far more of my family than I've heard of yours. Do you have brothers? Sisters?"

Deeply touched that he would want to know more about her, and heartened, too, that she'd managed to engage him, Nora nonetheless felt a wave of sadness. "No brothers. It was only my twin sister and me…Kristina, but she died last summer not long after our mother. A fever came upon them…"

She didn't say more, her throat tightening even as Niall's embrace grew tighter around her.

"See, woman? You've suffered, too. My parents died long ago from illness as well. Hearts break as deeply from such loss as from betrayal."

Now it was Nora who sighed raggedly, nodding.

Aye, her heart had been broken when Kristina and her mother had died and never had truly mended...much like Niall though Triona had told her of his weeks spent in Ostmentown trying to drink away his rage and sorrow. Until last night when she had tripped over him where he lay upon the dock—

"Did your father remarry?"

Shocked out of her thoughts, Nora gave an involuntary shudder. "Aye, to Agnes. My father is a good man but mayhap his grief allowed him to be swayed by her. It was Agnes's plan that her Norse cousin Sigurd wed Kristina for the alliance it would bring, but when she died..."

Nora fell silent and lowered her head, finding it still so difficult to talk about her sister's death. Yet Niall gently lifted her chin to face him.

"You became the innocent lamb to take her place."

Nora nodded, Niall staring at her so intently now that she felt her face growing hot. Her breath coming faster. Her heart beating hard against her breast.

How could he do that to her so easily? Ah, but even as she asked herself that question, Nora knew the answer.

She had fallen deeply, irrevocably in love with her husband, Niall O'Byrne.

"Say you forgive me, Nora," came his husky voice to make her heart race even faster. "I never meant to frighten you or to do anything to hurt you."

"But you didn't—" Niall's finger pressed gently to Nora's lips had silenced her, and she blinked at him in surprise.

"Aye, I did. Denied you a wedding feast. Left you alone and wondering what had become of me. Tried to drown myself in drink like a damned fool though I swear, wife, I will *never* resort to that madness again. Will you forgive me?"

His finger had fallen from her lips to caress her cheek, which made Nora feel as if she were melting inside. "Aye, Niall. I forgive you."

At once she felt some of the tension ease from his body though still, he held her so tightly.

Still, he stared so earnestly into her eyes.

"We'll do our best from this moment forward to forget the past and mend our hearts together. I want you to be happy, Nora. For *us* to be happy and I vow to make it so."

He rose abruptly with her from the chair, lifting Nora as if she weighed nothing at all while she flung her arms around his neck.

Her heart filled with hope, her spirits soaring, Nora already felt happier than she had ever imagined possible. As Niall strode with her to the door, she glanced around the candlelit room scented so sweetly with roses. "What of Maire? You said you were going to tell me about her."

"Aye, I did, and I'm grateful to know she's happy and

wed to the man she loves." Niall shoved open the door with his shoulder and stepped outside, grinning now. "Begorra, wife, we've plenty of time to talk of my sister later."

Shivering at his husky emphasis on 'later', Nora said nothing more as Niall strode with her toward his dwelling-house.

Aye, it would appear that she and Maire had much in common.

Nora was happy, too, indescribably, and married to the man she loved!

"So you say you saw a young woman running along the dock?"

"Aye, Lord Knutson!"

Sigurd squinted against the fiery setting sun and raised the Ostman's chin higher with the razor sharp blade of his axe. A yellow pool suddenly at his feet, he cursed roundly to see that the trembling fool had wet himself. "What else do you remember, man?"

"She stumbled, lord, and I heard her scream. God help me, I was so drunk I wasn't sure if I'd imagined it all! Yet I would swear she fell into the river...and then he dove in after her."

"*He?*"

"A stranger...aye, if it's the same man. Irish, not Ostman. Dark hair. Light eyes. He's fairly lived at the tavern for weeks though no sight of him since last night.

God help them, mayhap he and that poor woman both drowned—"

"*Jump.*"

Sweat dripping from his brow, the man stared at Sigurd in confusion. "Lord?"

"Jump now or die!"

The man took two steps backward on the dock and obliged him, launching himself into the River Liffey and carried downstream at once—while Sigurd's violent oath rent the air.

With that swift current, Nora would have been carried out to sea in moments…unless the man who had dove in after her had managed to catch her first.

Catch her and swim with her to the riverbank somewhere to the east of where Sigurd stood now, the ramshackle tavern emptied of its bleary-eyed patrons so he could question each and every one of them.

So he had done along the vast dock at every drinking house until he'd finally found someone who had seen a woman Sigurd believed deep in his bones had been his reluctant bride. By Odin, at last some news of her! He leveled his axe now and peered above the polished blade to the east while a couple of the drunken sots awaiting his questioning had actually begun to weep.

"Silence!"

As the weeping instantly stopped except for some pitiful hiccoughing, Sigurd focused once again upon the distant Irish Sea. At first light tomorrow his four hundred men would begin to search that span for any sign that Nora and her rescuer had dragged themselves from the river.

His instincts screamed to him that she was still alive…and his instincts had never been wrong.

He had only to find her and wed her…and then he vowed that Nora MacTorkil would forever rue the day she had fled from Sigurd Skullcrusher.

CHAPTER 10

"What do you think, Nora O'Byrne? Shall we arise or stay abed?"

Drawing her closer against him, Niall wasn't surprised that his whisper drew no more than a sleepy sigh from Nora as he nuzzled the silky nape of her neck. After all, he'd kept her up for a good part of the night until exhaustion had overwhelmed both of them.

He smiled to himself, breathing in the warm lavender scent of her skin.

He hadn't felt such peace in weeks. With Nora nestled in his arms, her sweetly rounded bottom flush against his hips, it was so easy to forget for a while everything that lay outside of this big bed.

Their bed. *Their* home…and one day, that of their children, too. Mayhap they had already made a babe together, he and his bride, which made him press a fervent kiss beneath her ear. It was right and good that it be so, just as he'd accepted that it was right and good that Nora gaze at him with love shining in her eyes from the moment they had left Maire's dwelling-house together.

Triona had been right. Nora had opened her heart to him…and he had vowed to himself deep in the night to open his heart to her as well.

If not love yet, he could not deny that he felt such an intense desire to cherish and protect her that the depths of such emotion had shaken him.

For Nora to have come to him so bravely yesterday…not knowing what she would find and wanting nothing more than to offer him comfort, had bonded Niall to her more completely than he would have thought possible.

In truth his memories of Caitlin were growing dim compared to Nora's gentleness and tender heart, which made him press a kiss to the delicate shell of her ear.

"Will you not wake, wife? Mayhap you need another way for me to rouse you."

Niall drew her closer, his shaft growing hard at once as she instinctively pushed her lush bottom against him—and he knew then that she was awake. She trembled, too, her flesh dimpling with goosebumps, and it wasn't because he'd thrown off the blankets to the foot of the bed when he'd first awoke.

He had wanted to gaze upon her, this woman whose lithe body was the very image of perfection, her tousled auburn hair so dark and lovely against the creaminess of her skin.

Niall had always been a man partial to blondes, but now he thought of last night when she had straddled his hips and rode him, her beautiful breasts bobbing and her long hair cascading down her back. In the candlelight her lustrous blue eyes had mesmerized him, though she kept them closed now even as her dusky eyelashes fluttered.

The air in the room seemed charged with anticipation, and Niall saw too, that her breasts rose and fell faster with her breathing. He smiled and slid his hand along the lush curve of her hip, his lower body growing harder still.

So hard that he could wait no longer as he entered her from behind, the tight warmth of her body making him suck in his breath.

She felt so wet that he could not help nipping her shoulder even as his fingers slipped between her thighs to find the swollen nub hidden in her slick woman's folds.

Now she sucked in her breath, too, moving against him as he thrust inside her slowly, languorously…but not for long. When her fingers laced with his own to ply along with him the nub that pulsed now beneath his touch, he had never felt so aroused. He began to thrust harder as she bucked in his arms, but he held her fast, his restraint making her moan.

Her unbridled movement made him groan, his body shaking now as he buried his face in her neck, her hair, and spurted his burning seed deep inside her with one last powerful thrust.

"Nora…"

As if from some faraway place she heard Niall moan her name, Nora blinded by the lightning flashing across her eyelids as her body suddenly went rigid.

The fierce throbbing of his flesh propelled her to the very edge of a precipice until the circling pressure of his fingers made her shudder in ecstasy against him.

"Oh God, Niall!"

When she fluttered open her eyes moments later, Niall held her close, his breathing still hard at her neck although he managed a low husky laugh.

"Woman…with mornings like this I won't have any strength left to leave our bed."

Nora laughed softly, too, but in truth, she never wanted to leave their bed.

To have Niall holding her with his arms so tight around her and his male flesh still deep inside her was a wonder unlike anything she'd known…or had ever hoped to know.

Her heart felt so full to overflowing that she had no words with which to speak. Instead she nestled contentedly against him and delighted in the warmth of his breath fanning her ear.

"You're a temptress, Nora O'Byrne, did you know that? To nuzzle so against me…"

His fervent kiss at her nape made her shiver, and she wondered with her face suddenly burning if more lovemaking lay in store. She found her answer at once when she felt him swell harder within her.

She had astonished herself that she delighted so much in the pleasure they shared together, and she wondered, too, if Niall might have been surprised by her wild abandon. If so, he hadn't seemed at all to mind—

"Niall? Nora? Are you awake?"

Triona's voice calling to them from the adjoining room made Nora gasp in surprise while Niall grabbed for the blankets heaped at the foot of the bed. They had barely covered themselves before Triona shamelessly peeked her head inside the door, a radiant smile lighting her face.

"Aye, now, isn't that a fine sight! You'll have to forgive me, but I had to see for myself that all was well and so it is…the two of you all snuggled together—"

"Triona O'Byrne!" In mock anger, Niall balled up a down pillow and threw it across the room, though Triona dodged the missile and only laughed.

"Dawn was hours ago! Time to rise, we've so much to do! Nora, the seamstresses are waiting to measure you even now for your new gowns and I want you to meet little Deirdre—oh no, Conn!"

Nora shrieked as a gangly gray wolfhound bounded past Triona into the room and jumped into the middle of the bed, immediately straddling Niall to lick his face.

As Niall began to laugh, stroking the shaggy beast affectionately, Nora was certain she was next for the friendly greeting as Conn plopped down between her and Niall. Only Triona's shrill whistle made the huge dog jump from the bed and he was out the door again before Nora could even blink.

"Well, now you've met my brave Conn the Hundred Fighter," Triona said, grinning as she shrugged her shoulders. "There's Maeve the Warrior-Queen, too—"

"Her cat," Niall interjected, shifting closer to Nora again. "All of her pets are named after Éire's ancient heroes."

"And Ferdiad," Triona added.

Now Niall grinned at Nora, too. "Her falcon. Maeve's Connaught champion and both friend and foe to the mighty warrior Cuchulain."

"Aye, and don't forget Laeg!"

"Her stallion named after Cuchulain's stalwart charioteer. A magnificent beast."

"You ride a stallion?" Nora breathed in awe, realizing there was much she hadn't learned yet about her amazing sister-in-law.

"Aye, as often as I can...though Ronan isn't too pleased about it now that I'm with child several months. Yet when else might I forego these silly gowns to wear trousers? I'll have the seamstresses make you several pair...but nothing will get done until the two of you get out of bed!"

With that Triona disappeared out the door, her lighthearted voice calling to them from the other room, "There's food out here for you...toasted oat bread and honey and some freshly smoked salmon. Nora, I'll see you soon at the sewing house!"

Nora glanced at Niall, so astonished she didn't know what to say though her stomach suddenly grumbled, while he threw back his head and laughed.

"They're searching the riverbank very near to us, I see them!"

"Aye, Father Edmund, a sad business indeed." Father Gilbert shook his bald head as he lingered over his midday meal of salted pork and boiled eggs. "Lord Knutson's time is wasted, I fear. Magnus MacTorkil's daughter Nora has surely drowned—ah, no sense in letting my food grow cold to discuss it further. Come away from the window and pour me more wine!"

Savoring another mouthful, Father Gilbert wiped sticky egg yolk from his fat fingers with a linen cloth as the old priest shuffled forward to oblige him. Yet he sighed with exasperation when Father Edmund's gnarled hands shook while refilling his polished silver cup.

"My brother, what has stirred you so? Are you ill?"

"Mayhap very soon more than ill," Father Gilbert heard his brother priest mutter as if to himself, but then Father Edmund withdrew from the table and hastened back to the window. Father Gilbert merely shrugged and took a long draft of red wine, smacking his lips.

If the commotion along the river had captured the old priest's attention, what of it? Father Gilbert had to agree it was an uncommon thing to have hundreds of Norse warriors searching for a young woman whose recklessness and folly had surely cost the poor soul her life.

He could not fathom why Lord Knutson believed Nora MacTorkil yet alive, but mayhap wounded pride was driving him to that conclusion. Either that or the startling news that some fool had attempted to rescue her and had dove into the River Liffey after her had given the jilted bridegroom false hope. Those strong currents were known to be deadly to even the strongest of swimmers…aye, it was an unpleasant business all the way around.

With a hearty belch, Father Gilbert rose from the table and glanced with mounting exasperation at his brother priest who craned his scrawny neck out the window. If he was not mistaken, he would swear the old man was shaking from head to foot.

"Come, Father Edmund, let us go into the sanctuary for much prayer is needed. Lord Sigurd Knutson may claim himself a Christian, but it's clear he holds fast to his pagan beliefs as well, may God forgive him. I've never heard such blasphemous oaths to Odin as last night when he swore in Lord MacTorkil's hall that he wouldn't rest until he found his bride, drowned or alive!"

Father Gilbert didn't wait for his brother priest, who hadn't turned from the window, but shrugged again and made his way to the doorway leading into the church.

A pity that such a brilliantly sunny day would be spent looking for a bloated corpse. Aye, indeed, there was much to pray about—

"What…?" Father Gilbert stopped in his tracks at the glitter of gold in the corner and something else. Something a sparkling blue…

"Father Edmund, do you see that?" Father Gilbert heard the old man turn from the window, but he had already knelt heavily on one knee to retrieve a gold filigree ring from the floor.

A gold filigree ring with a blue sapphire that glittered in the sunlight spilling into the room as Father Gilbert felt his heart seem to stop.

He knew this ring! He had seen it last summer at the deathbed of Kristina MacTorkil, when the dying young woman had given the ring to her twin sister, Nora. Yet how had it come to be in his living quarters?

A terrible sinking feeling gripped him even as he turned slowly and met Father Edmund's panicked eyes. The old priest's face looked so deathly pale that Father Gilbert already had his answer.

"She's been here...Nora MacTorkil," he breathed, incredulous. "She didn't drown after all—"

"Ah, God, we must flee before they get here!" Father Edmund broke in, wringing his hands. "We must flee!"

Father Gilbert knew exactly who the stricken priest meant as cold fear suddenly gripped him. In the distance from the direction of the river he could hear raised men's voices that told him dried footprints must have been found. Even worse, mayhap a telltale path of crushed weeds and grass led to the church as, dear God in heaven, one man's familiar voice bellowed above the rest.

Lord Knutson.

Sigurd Skullcrusher.

Crossing himself, Father Gilbert knew with dead certainty, too, that Father Edmund had a gripping tale to confess, but now was not the time nor place.

Not if they both wanted to live another day and not find themselves hacked to pieces by an enraged Norseman's axe or impaled upon a spear outside the church for all to see.

"To the stable, Father Edmund, now!" Hastening as fast as his girth would allow him, his meal churning in his stomach, Father Gilbert fled with his brother priest into the church and down the aisle to the narthex.

Their only hope lay in reaching Lord MacTorkil's stronghold before Sigurd Knutson and his men caught up with them. They had one horse between them, thankfully a young swift animal…and only then did it dawn upon Father Gilbert what must have happened to the gelding that Father Edmund had said escaped from his stall two nights ago.

Aye, the old priest had much to confess, but not now. *Not now!*

Once outside the church Father Gilbert didn't dare glance toward the river for fear that the Norsemen were almost upon them. Yet Father Edmund's sharp intake of breath made his blood run cold, telling him that their flight had been noticed.

With Nora MacTorkil's ring clutched in his hand, Father Gilbert hoisted his priest's robe to his knees and ran for dear life toward the stable.

CHAPTER 11

"May I borrow my bride, Triona? You've already had her since morning while I'd like to at last spend some time with her."

Niall didn't receive any answer but a squeal from Deirdre and laughter from Triona and Nora as both women swung the delighted child between them. In truth, he could have stood there in Ronan and Triona's dwelling-house watching the happy troupe much longer, Nora's cheeks flushed pink and her smile radiant.

A smile that upon seeing her again after hours spent apart Niall couldn't deny had clutched at his heart, astonishing him.

He had never seen his new wife look lovelier than in her pale yellow gown, her stunning blue eyes alight and her laughter so merry.

How far she had come in so short a time from the terrified woman he had dragged from the river, but Niall thrust that black thought at once from his mind.

He didn't want to think about the discussion he'd just had with Ronan, either, his brother pressing him again about the Norse warrior Sigurd Knutson though Niall had already told him everything he knew.

Aye, he shared Ronan's unease that Father Edmund might forswear his oath, but what else could Niall do but continue praying that the old priest held his tongue? All Niall wanted to concern himself with now was that he and Nora were moving forward together, that unhappy past hopefully behind them…which was why he'd come to find her.

He had a surprise in store for her…a ride from the stronghold to one of his favorite places in Glenmalure. That is, if he could steal Nora's attention from little Deirdre, who clasped her chubby arms around Nora's neck.

Seeing his bride with the beautiful child clutched at his heart too, Niall suddenly overcome with an intense longing for a family, which he'd never felt before.

How his life had changed, too, in so short a time. Once more he silently vowed to open his heart to his wife who threw him a brilliant smile that stilled his breath.

Begorra, mayhap he didn't need to open his heart…but had done so already, Niall thought as Nora hastened toward him with the laughing child in her arms.

"Oh, Niall, we've had such a wonderful time!"

He smiled back at her, and at once Deirdre reached out to him for a hug. He wrapped both of them in a big embrace, while Triona's laughter filled the sunny room.

"I always knew you'd make a fine family man, Niall O'Byrne! Mayhap in nine months or so Deirdre will have another playmate besides the babe I carry! Did you say you wanted to steal Nora away from us for a while?"

"Aye, if she'll agree to it," Niall teased, noting Nora's deep blush though her eyes shone with happiness. "Will you come for a ride with me, wife?"

She nodded, but before she could say a word Triona hastened forward to retrieve her wriggling daughter.

"Go on, the both of you, while there's plenty of daylight. This wee one needs her nap while I've only three days to make sure your wedding feast is the finest we've seen in Glenmalure!" Already Triona was heading with Deirdre to the adjoining room, although she called over her shoulder, "You've a fitting for your new gowns first thing tomorrow, Nora, don't forget. Aye, and your trousers!"

"No, no, I won't—oh!"

Niall had swept her into his arms before she could linger another moment and strode with her to the door.

Nora looked so astonished, which made him grin broadly as he stepped outside with her into the early afternoon sunshine.

"Sometimes a man must resort to drastic measures to have his wife all to himself, but if you'd rather go back—"

"Don't even think of it, Niall O'Byrne!" She grinned at him now, too, and threw her arms around his neck to hug him tightly, which made Niall stride all the faster toward the stable.

"Oh, Niall, it's so beautiful here!" Very much aware of his arm around her waist as they stood side by side, Nora gazed with him at the sunlight sparkling upon the surface of the lough.

It hadn't been that far of a ride from the O'Byrne stronghold, but she would never have guessed that a mountain lake lay beyond a rise, sheltered by a thick stand of fir trees. She felt awestruck by the bright blue of the water reflecting a cloudless summer sky, but it was the tumultuous roar of a waterfall that fed the lake that took her breath away.

She had never traveled far from her father's stronghold in Ostmentown, so she had never before seen anything as magnificent as this glittering jewel of a lough flanked by rugged peaks. Niall had said only that he was taking her to one of his favorite places, and she could see why.

Smiling, she glanced up at him to find him looking at her now, Niall from his own broad smile clearly pleased by her delight.

They had left their mount, Niall's mighty dappled gray stallion, grazing upon grass near the trees and had walked together to the edge of the lough. As Niall turned to face her, Nora felt her heart begin to pound.

He looked so earnest all of a sudden as he pulled a cloth pouch from his sword belt. She had never before seen him armed other than with his knife, but she understood that was the way of things for an O'Byrne rebel when venturing outside the stronghold. In the bright sunlight he looked so formidable and strong, yet his gaze held tenderness as he dumped something out of the pouch into his hand and held it out to her.

A delicate gold band with an oval garnet that shone blood red in the sunlight.

"My mother's ring…and her mother's before her. I had no ring to give you when we wed, but now this one is yours."

"Niall…" Nora could but breathe his name, she felt so moved as he lifted her left hand and slipped the ring on her fourth finger. Tears clouded her eyes that the band fit her so perfectly.

The lough one of his favorite places. His mother's ring. Was it possible he felt a stirring of emotion for her now that hadn't been there before? Hope soaring in her heart, she lifted her face to him as he bent his head to kiss her.

Not hungrily as he had done during the night but gently, his lips so warm upon hers, stilling her breath. Would the wondrous turn her life had taken never cease to amaze her?

Then he was smiling as he pulled her into his arms, and once again his mouth found hers. This time his kiss wasn't so gentle but achingly possessive…while she felt as if she were melting against him, her hands splayed out upon his powerful chest, his heartbeat so strong and steady beneath her fingers.

She hadn't worn such a beautiful ring since the one Kristina had given her—*ah, no, why would she think of that now?*

Niall must have sensed her sudden tension for he drew back to study her face.

"Nora?"

Tears blinded her again...and she thought wildly of telling him that very moment about her blue sapphire ring and her desperate prayers that it had sunk to the bottom of the River Liffey.

Niall had seen her arm-rings and jeweled brooch yesterday in their dwelling-house when he had stripped her of everything she wore and then carried her to the bed. She had wanted to tell him then about the ring Kristina had given her and how it was missing.

Yet she'd feared by even voicing the words, somehow she might invite terrible calamity upon them. After all they had only begun to taste happiness together! So she had forced all such thoughts away when he had begun to kiss her lips, her throat, her breasts—

"Nora, is it the water? It wasn't my thought that we would swim...just to come here together."

"A-aye, the water," she lied, feeling terrible in doing so but loathe even more now to tell him the truth. She would not think of her sister's ring again! All danger was past...it had to be! "Niall, forgive me, it's so lovely here...but it's so soon after the river. Too soon. I-I think we should go."

"Begorra, wife, we can't have such dark memories plaguing our life. Our future."

He'd spoken so gently to her, drawing her against him to nuzzle her cheek, her ear, but then he released her and stepped back as his hands went to his sword belt.

Already the small pouch that had carried his mother's ring lay at his feet, Nora's eyes widening as his leather sword belt soon followed. The next thing she knew he had pulled his tunic over his head, his magnificent upper torso now bared to her gaze.

"Niall…what?"

She realized as soon as he kicked off his boots what he had in mind, a blush burning her face even before he began to pull off his trousers. Then, as naked as God had created him, he stepped from the sloping bank into the shallow water and reached out his hand to her.

"Come for a swim with me, Nora O'Byrne. We'll face this demon today and put it forever behind us."

Oh, God, she wanted to cry out that there was another demon…a terrible seven-foot-tall demon with a pox-scarred face, cruel eyes, and a broad axe that could cleave a man in two who might still threaten their happiness. She had no doubt a search had been called for her. Father Edmund might well hold fast to his vow, but if that sapphire ring had slipped from the pouch at the church to prove she had been there—

"Very well, then, I'll carry you in myself."

"No, Niall, wait!" Nora kicked off her leather slippers and then with trembling fingers, she reached down to grab the hem of her yellow silk gown so she might pull it up over her head. Her hair was so thick that the fabric caught at her chin, covering her face, and she began to struggle until she felt Niall's strong hands grasp hers.

Within an instant she was divested of her gown and standing there in her sheer white camise, while he stared into her flushed face, grinning.

"You really don't want to swim, do you?"

He didn't wait for her answer, but lifted her into his arms and walked with her knee-deep into the lough. Only then did he set her down and swiftly strip the thin camise from her body and toss it onto the bank.

"Take my hands, Nora. I promise I won't let anything happen to you."

She obliged him, the water not as cool as she had imagined it might be, mayhap because the day was so sunny and warm.

As he walked backward into deeper water, his gaze, riveted upon her as he pulled her along with him, made her shiver nonetheless. She had come to know that hungry look in his eyes that told her his thoughts had strayed far from swimming.

So had her thoughts strayed, too, all else mercifully forgotten as shoulder-deep in the lough now, he drew her against him. Her feet no longer touched the pebbly bottom, but they didn't need to as Niall spun her around and leaned back to begin swimming with her atop him.

One heavily muscled arm beneath her breasts, her wet nipples taut and pointed to the sky, while his other arm powerfully moved them through the water.

"You see, wife? We're swimming. Nothing to fear."

His husky voice did anything but soothe her, and she felt then underneath her bottom that it wasn't just her nipples that had grown so hard. The deeper water felt colder now, which made her tremble...or mayhap it was that with his every stroke she felt the muscular strength of his body beneath her. She laid her head back against his shoulder and attempted to relax, but how could she?

Nora gasped. His hand cupped her breast now, his fingernails grazing a sensitive nipple even as he began to swim with her toward shore.

Not in so leisurely a fashion any longer but with powerful strokes that churned the water around them, and she grew breathless though she hadn't exerted herself one wee bit.

As soon as his feet touched bottom, he swept her into his arms and strode with her dripping wet to the grassy bank, where he laid her down and blanketed her body with his own.

She welcomed him with open arms and spread her thighs beneath him, his turgid flesh sinking into her even as she cried out and locked her legs around his hips.

Her calves against his taut buttocks pressing him deeper with his every thrust.

His mouth capturing hers as she cried out again, shaking uncontrollably, her climax meeting his with such force that she could not say where his impassioned groans began and hers ended.

All she knew moments later when he lay so spent atop her, both of them breathing hard, her legs still locked around him, was that she liked swimming with Niall very much indeed.

That thought made her giggle, which made him laugh, too, as if he'd read her mind. A deep rumbling sound that echoed around the lough as he rolled over with her so that she lay atop him, her long wet hair covering them like a veil.

"Aye, woman, while it's warm, I believe we'll be swimming here a lot. Agreed?"

He raised his head to kiss her soundly before she could say a word, while Nora cradled his face and kissed him right back, which was answer enough for her.

CHAPTER 12

"You burned down the church?" Magnus MacTorkil stared in disbelief at the smoldering ruins while Sigurd Knutson swore vehemently and spat with disgust at the ground.

"A foul crime happened there, MacTorkil! What else could I be expected to do? That damned Father Edmund wed my promised bride to another man!"

Now Magnus felt like he'd been struck at this unexpected news.

He had only just dismounted from his lathered horse, having ridden like the devil east of Ostmentown when he'd heard from some of his men that Sigurd was laying waste to the countryside. "Nora is alive?"

"Aye, she's alive and run off into the mountains with her husband, Niall O'Byrne!"

A sudden sharp pain made Magnus clutch at his chest. This astonishing news was too much, too much!

Struggling to catch his breath, he glanced around him at the grim faces of Sigurd's men…scores of them. More than Magnus would have ever imagined would cross the sea from Norway to witness a wedding. A whole army of Norsemen!

But now to learn that Nora was alive and married to an O'Byrne? A second pain gripped him, though not as intense as the first. God help him, he could not make sense of it!

"Where is Father Edmund?" Magnus rasped, still finding it hard to breathe. "I would speak to him—"

"Too late." With his axe, Sigurd indicated a charred corpse near what was once the front door of the church...no, two charred corpses, one larger than the first.

God in heaven, no, Father Edmund *and* Father Gilbert?

Sickened by the sight, aye, and the smell of burned flesh that suddenly assailed his nostrils, Magnus now felt rage rising inside him though he did his best to tamp it down.

He was a merchant, not a warrior! All the wealth he possessed and hoped yet to gain depended on his trade alliances with such ruthless men as Sigurd Knutson...though Magnus at that moment rejoiced that his daughter had been spared the fate of marrying this monster.

So Nora had called him, begging Magnus with desolate tears in her eyes to reconsider the marriage though he had turned a deaf ear to her.

How could he not what with Agnes's incessant harping? His shrewish second wife had threatened to make his life a misery if he did not fully support the match!

Magnus shuddered, wondering what Agnes would say at this surprising news. At least Nora hadn't drowned, but he still knew so little. Sigurd had left his side to approach one of the corpses. With a terrible howl, the enraged Norseman brought down his broad axe and buried the blade in what was left of poor Father Edmund.

Now Magnus did become sick, dropping to his knees to vomit upon the ground. As he wiped his mouth with the back of his hand, Sigurd's men began to jeer his weakness and beat their weapons upon their painted wooden shields.

"Get up, MacTorkil!"

Magnus began to rise but he wasn't fast enough for Sigurd, the hulking giant grasping him by the collar of his tunic and hauling him to his feet.

"Do you not wish to hear what I learned from those bastards before I set them aflame?"

Magnus nodded while Sigurd's face grew bright red, spittle foaming at the corners of his mouth.

"The two priests were fleeing to the stable, but my men caught them and dragged them to me. The fat one said he'd found this ring, Nora's ring! Do you recognize it?"

Again Magnus nodded at the blue sapphire ring sparkling in Sigurd's huge callused hand, until the Norseman clenched his fist around it.

"The old priest refused to say much at first—told me that he'd sworn a sacred vow not to utter a word of what had transpired until I threatened to cut the fat one's throat. Your daughter was carried near drowned to the church by this Niall O'Byrne, who must have been the man that dove from the dock to save her. He revived her and then decided to marry her. *My promised bride!*"

Shouts of derision erupted around them at Sigurd's words, his men once more striking their shields with intensifying fury. All it took was one wave from the huge Norseman to silence them. Sigurd grabbed Magnus by the front of his tunic and pulled him to within inches of his pox-marked face.

"Tell me of Niall O'Byrne! Who is he? Where will I find him?"

Magnus tried not to grimace, Sigurd's breath was so foul. "If it's the same man I know of, he's Tanist to his elder brother Ronan Black O'Byrne, chieftain of the Glenmalure O'Byrnes."

"Tanist?"

"Aye, he would succeed as chieftain if anything befell Black O'Byrne, a legendary rebel in Éire. The Normans fear him. Hate him and his clansmen for their fierce raiding against them."

"By Odin, how did Niall O'Byrne come to be in Ostmentown? The man who saw him jump into the river after my bride said he lived at a tavern for weeks! Others called him a drunkard—"

"I-I don't know, Lord Knutson...unless the rumor heard from Dublin was true."

"Rumor?"

"Aye, that the woman he was pledged to wed, the daughter of Donal MacMurrough, chose another and spurned him. Mayhap that drove him here to drink, to forget—ah, God!"

Sigurd had shoved him away so violently that Magnus fell backward to the ground, the Norseman towering over him.

"How far a march to Glenmalure?"

Sigurd's voice sunk to a growl, Magnus blanched at the axe hovering so close to his head. "Three days…but by horseback, mayhap less than a day if you know the land and ride hard. It's treacherous country. Mountainous. Dangerous. The rebel clans suffer no one trespassing upon their domain—"

"*I* fear no rebel clans! *We* fear no rebel clans!"

Sigurd's roar echoing around them, his axe now raised above his head, he turned to his men who roared right back at him and brandished their weapons.

"We march at dawn to retrieve my bride! I swear if these O'Byrnes refuse to give her over to me, we *will* destroy them!"

Sigurd spun back around and leveled his axe at Magnus's face. "When we return with your daughter to Ostmentown, you will send your swiftest ship to Rome to seek an annulment from the Pope for this heinous marriage. Do you understand me?"

Magnus nodded, the ominous blade hovering a mere inch from his nose, though a troubling thought suddenly occurred to him. "If the marriage has been consummated, Nora may already be with—"

"Silence!" His face mottled with rage, Sigurd bent down to hiss at Magnus, "What do I care if another man's seed bears fruit? When I sail home to Norway, I will have your gold, your daughter, and mayhap an heir I will claim as my own blood growing in her womb! Now get up!"

Shaking, Magnus struggled to his feet only to have Sigurd shove him toward his horse.

"Back to the stronghold, MacTorkil! There is much to prepare before dawn. We'll need wagons, horses, provisions! Summon as many of your men as are able to wield a sword to fight alongside us! Now go!"

Fierce shouts for vengeance rent the air as Magnus hauled himself atop his mount, though the fresh pain in his chest made him suck in his breath.

Yet it was nothing to the bitter regret stabbing at him for what he had done to Nora.

He had wronged her unforgivably, he knew that now as he kicked his horse into a gallop and left Sigurd and his raucous men and their murderous atrocity behind him.

Just as Magnus sensed, one hand clutching at his chest, that he was dying. Was there nothing at this terrible juncture that he could do to help her?

"Oh, Triona, it's so beautiful! I've never worn anything finer!"

Nora spun around with excitement as the shimmering white silk of her gown caught the afternoon sunshine streaming in the windows, while the seamstresses oohed and aahed at their handiwork. A lavender overdress with a matching white silk bodice and appliqued sleeves completed the gown, which was unlike anything Nora had ever seen before.

Even Deirdre propped on Triona's hip clapped her chubby hands with delight.

The half dozen new gowns that Nora had been fitted for yesterday hung finished as well in a dazzling array of colors in one corner of the sewing house. Aye, but this white and lavender one was the gown she had chosen to wear to the wedding feast tomorrow night. She couldn't wait!

"Do you think Niall will like it?" Nora glanced over her shoulder at Triona, who handed Deirdre to a maidservant come to fetch the child for her afternoon nap.

"Like it? You're as lovely a new bride as I've ever seen, Nora O'Byrne...hmm, but how shall we dress your hair? Would you like to wear a veil? A wreath of wildflowers?"

"Aye, wildflowers," Nora murmured, indeed feeling truly beautiful for the first time in her life. Did happiness make it so? Being so in love with her husband that she felt her heart might burst just in thinking of him?

They had parted this morning when Niall, Ronan, and a host of clansmen had left the stronghold to hunt deer and wild boar for the feast. Already Nora felt like it had been a lifetime since she'd seen him. Did he miss her, too? She glanced down at the garnet ring he had given her at the lough, a symbol she now felt certain was of his growing feelings for her.

If what Triona claimed at yesterday's fitting was true, that Niall had been so reluctant to leave Nora at the sewing house that he couldn't but be falling in love with her, then aye, he missed her!

"Thinking of Niall?" Triona teased her as several seamstresses rushed forward to help Nora out of the gown. "You're blushing again."

So she was, Nora realized, her face flushed with warmth. How could she not think constantly of Niall when he had become everything to her...her love, her life, her breath? Her smile seemed answer enough for Triona, who laughed and hastened to her side to hug her.

"I'm so pleased to have another sister! I pray every night that someday we'll see Maire again. You would love her just as I do."

Nora saw at once the wistfulness in Triona's eyes, and nodded. "I'll pray for that day, too."

"Good. With both of us praying, that day will come, I know it!" With a soft sigh, Triona gestured to one of the seamstresses. "Now for the last fitting. Have you ever worn trousers before?"

"No, never." Nora laughed nervously, not sure what to think as a stout older woman came forward with a pair of brown trousers draped over her arm.

"Go on, Nora, try them on!" Triona urged her, standing back now with her hands on her hips. "The trousers won't bite you, I promise."

Nora did, slipping first one leg and then the other into the unfamiliar garment and then tucking in her camise, while Triona whooped with delight.

"I could never convince Maire to wear them even when

I was teaching her to ride, but look at you! They fit you perfectly!"

Nora turned this way and that, eyeing the trousers skeptically. They felt comfortable enough, but yet so strange. As Triona beckoned to her, Nora took a few steps toward her beaming sister-in-law.

"Aye, you can walk freely and run freely and ride like the wind without a ridiculous gown to fetter you. What do you think?"

Nora laughed to herself, shaking her head in amazement. "I...I like them!"

"Of course you like them! Now try this shirt and leather jerkin, too, and here's a pair of my shoes I'll loan to you until we have some made for you."

Within moments Nora was dressed wholly unlike she'd ever been before, while Triona grinned from ear-to-ear and appeared quite pleased with herself.

"We'll look like twins, Nora! The next time Ronan and Niall go hunting, we'll wear our trousers and ride along with them so you can feel the difference for yourself. You'll never want to wear a gown atop a horse again!"

Triona's delight was so infectious that Nora smiled too, though she felt a twinge of sadness thinking of her real twin, Kristina. Once they had laughed together and tried on new gowns together—

"Jesu, Mary, and Joseph, I think I hear them riding into the stronghold now, but it's too early. They weren't expected back until dark."

Grateful to be wrested from her melancholy thoughts,

Nora nonetheless felt alarm that Triona looked so concerned. "Is something wrong?"

"I don't know yet. Come on!"

Nora gasped as Triona grabbed her hand and together they hurried from the sewing house.

Aye, it was true, Nora had never felt such freedom of movement as in her new trousers when they ran toward the opened gates, though Triona had to hold up her gown with her free hand.

Yet Nora forgot altogether about what she wore at the commotion and fierce shouting all around them. Her heart leapt into her throat when she spied Niall jumping down from his lathered stallion to rush toward her.

"Niall?"

He said nothing but propelled her in the opposite direction as Ronan roared out above the din, "Everyone into the feasting-hall! Now!"

CHAPTER 13

"Sigurd Knutson is marching upon Glenmalure?" Shaking her head in disbelief, Nora felt as if she couldn't breathe.

She stood with Niall and Triona near the huge hearth, along with the several hundred O'Byrne clansmen, women, and children behind them who had rushed to the feasting-hall at Ronan's command.

All eyes were glued to their chieftain, faces grim, any crying from babes shushed at once as an air of foreboding hung over the massive room.

The Ostman standing next to Ronan, whom Nora recognized as one of her father's personal guards, looked half dead from exhaustion, he'd ridden so hard to reach them. *Dear God, to warn them.* Ronan and Niall and their clansmen had come upon him not far from the stronghold, their hunt so successful they had turned early toward home.

"Go on, man!" Ronan urged him after offering a cup of wine that the Ostman downed in one swallow. Drawing in a deep ragged breath, he rushed on.

"Lord Knutson and his men are making camp for the night in Glendalough. The wagons with provisions could go no further over such rough terrain. Lord MacTorkil seized upon the commotion to send me here, God help him that no one noticed."

"How many men?" Ronan demanded.

"Four hundred…along with a hundred or more Ostmen summoned by Lord MacTorkil."

A sudden rumble of voices and sharp curses among the O'Byrnes went up at that number, but Ronan waved his hand for silence.

"Magnus MacTorkil marches upon us as well and yet he sent you here to warn us?"

"Aye, my lord, he had no choice. Lord Knutson learned from a priest two days past that his promised bride, Nora MacTorkil, is among you. He has vowed to have her back or he will destroy you."

Fierce shouts erupted now among the O'Byrnes, clenched fists and brandished swords raised high in the air. Nora was certain her knees might give way beneath her, she felt so sickened, so stunned. The only thing that kept her standing was Niall drawing her against him, his arm firmly around her waist.

"Not MacTorkil but Nora O'Byrne!" he roared above the melee, his expression furious. "No man shall take my bride from me! Not Sigurd Knutson! *No one!*"

Again Ronan had to wave for silence, but it took longer now to quiet the gathered throng. Nora felt the O'Byrnes' mounting defiance like a live thing in the feasting-hall, which helped to bolster her. That, and Triona reaching over to squeeze her hand.

"This priest was the one that married my brother and his wife?" Ronan queried the Ostman in a harsh voice that once more made the feasting-hall grow still.

"Aye, Father Edmund, but he was slain along with Father Gilbert, who found a ring at the church that proved Nora MacTor—O'Byrne hadn't drowned. Lord Knutson was so incensed to hear of the marriage that he cut their throats and set their bodies ablaze…and torched the church as well."

Now Nora's knees did give way, but Niall caught her and swept her into his arms. His gaze burned into hers.

"A ring, Nora?"

She nodded, her throat so tight she could hardly speak. "I…I prayed it had been lost in the river. I wanted to tell you, truly…but I could not. I was so afraid. Forgive me."

He embraced her so tightly then and kissed her brow that Nora knew with immense relief that he didn't blame her. Yet his expression still looked so grave, no doubt Niall thinking about Father Edmund just as she couldn't believe the old priest had been brutally murdered.

"Enough! Give the man some food and a place to rest!" Ronan commanded, his expression grown even darker than Niall's. "Clansmen, we prepare for battle! Sigurd Knutson and his Norsemen will be upon us tomorrow!"

"Nora, stay with Triona!" Niall bade her as he set her on the ground. For a brief moment he held her close, kissing her forehead and then lifting her chin to press his lips to hers, and then he was gone to join Ronan.

Nora stared after him, her heart aching, her mind spinning, until she started when she felt Triona squeeze her arm.

Tears bit Nora's eyes as she met Triona's gaze. Such gut-wrenching pain gripped her that she lay at the heart of this nightmare threatening Niall, his clansmen, their innocent wives and children—

"No, do not think it, Nora, not for another moment!" Triona told her fiercely as if reading Nora's mind. "You're an O'Byrne and we protect our own! Now come with me. There is much for all of us to do!"

Hours later and well past dusk, Nora had never known such exhaustion as Triona pushed open the door to her and Niall's dwelling-house. The torchlit yard beyond them was still filled with people rushing to and fro, dogs barking, and occasional shouts, though Nora hadn't seen Niall since the gathering in the feasting-hall. Longing for him, she sighed and stepped inside the door.

"Get some rest, Nora, that's all we can do now until morning."

She nodded as Triona gave her a quick hug, and then closed the door behind her.

Nora had wanted to do more, had begged Triona that she might remain with her to do more, but Triona had insisted firmly that Nora had more than done her part.

Alone now, her head spun from the number of storehouses she and Triona had visited to ensure all foodstuffs were in order for a potential siege. Then there had been the overseeing of linens cut and stacked for bandages. Last, they had made sure that the huge ovens in the kitchen flanking the feasting-hall were filled continuously with loaves of bread baking and the smokehouses stocked with dressed meat from the day's hunt.

Not for a wedding feast…but an impending battle the mere thought of which cut Nora to the quick. She forced herself to move further into the room, certain that if she remained by the door she would crumple there.

All was empty and quiet, only a few lamps lit by the maidservants who had left a simple meal of bread and salted meat upon the table, and two cups filled with ale.

Nora felt no hunger, but she stopped to take a few sips of ale to soothe her thirst. She looked around the room at the furnishings Niall had told her only this morning that she could arrange however she wanted, and to adorn their home as she saw fit with tapestries and carpets and anything she wished. He wanted her to be happy and comfortable here—ah, God!

Nora grasped the table for support, feeling again as if her knees might buckle beneath her. So many times while she had accompanied Triona from place to place these past hours, she had begun to tremble at the thought that Sigurd Skullcrusher and his men were so close to Glenmalure.

So close. Mayhap they were already making their way

here in the dark. The moon was still ripe, though waning, casting plenty of light upon the countryside—no, God, no, she couldn't think of it!

Suddenly feeling she must lie down or once more risk collapsing to the floor, Nora ran into the adjoining room and threw herself upon the bed.

Her and Niall's bed. She had no strength left to change out of her shirt and trousers, but only flung off the leather jerkin and kicked off her borrowed pair of shoes. Then she curled herself up into a tight ball and stared blindly at the wall.

She had no tears to weep, nor did she wish to. Weeping would gain her nothing, nor change the horror that tomorrow might bring.

The only small comfort she clung to was that her father had sent one of his men to warn them. She still could not believe it! What had caused his change of heart that he had sought to protect her in mayhap the only way he could?

"Oh, Niall…where are you?" Her broken whisper brought her no answer, and she closed her eyes against her mounting heartache.

She still felt so terrible that she hadn't told him about the sapphire ring, but there was no undoing it no matter how deeply she wished she could.

He was her husband to trust with whatever good or ill she might have to tell him, yet she'd said nothing! Her confession might have bought them a few more days to prepare for whatever calamity they faced tomorrow!

Now tears did come, but Nora forced them back.

Instead she prayed for sleep to rescue her...if only for a while from the bleak thoughts tumbling through her mind.

"Go home to your wife, Niall. We've done everything we can tonight."

Niall snorted at Ronan. "What? And leave you here to shoulder this weight alone? I'll go only if you make your way home to Triona."

Ronan didn't respond, but his heavy sigh told Niall much, aye, that his brother was thinking of his wife and daughter in the face of approaching battle.

God help them, an army of five hundred men marching upon Glenmalure!

Norsemen and Ostmen, fierce fighters all...though according to Magnus MacTorkil's man who'd ridden to warn them, Nora's father bore no sense of allegiance any longer to Sigurd Knutson.

Too late! What could one hundred Ostmen do to challenge four hundred Norse warriors that followed so ruthless a leader as Sigurd Knutson...no, *Sigurd Skullcrusher*?

So Niall and Ronan and their clansmen had debated this past hour, but no conclusion had been reached other than that tomorrow they would face overwhelming odds.

No such force had ever marched into Glenmalure! The O'Byrne stronghold had proved impregnable against smaller numbers, but one so large?

Finally Ronan had sent his clansmen away to their homes except Niall, though all of them would take turns manning the gates to keep watch during the night. The cover of darkness had always been an ally to them during their raids against the Normans…so why wouldn't their enemy attempt to use the same ploy to their advantage?

Niall's vehement curse broke the heavy silence in the feasting-hall, the fire in the great hearth only embers now and sputtering.

"Forgive me, Ronan. I would not have done anything differently…yet I judged from the moment I wed Nora that such a day might come."

Staring into the fire, Ronan said nothing and Niall said no more, though he sensed no blame from his brother.

No, not even when they had surrounded the exhausted Ostman near the stronghold and the man had blurted his ominous news.

Now Niall was the one that sighed heavily, while Ronan leaned forward in his chair to stare intently at him instead of the fire.

"Do you love this woman, Niall?"

Niall wasn't surprised that Ronan would ask him such a question at this dark hour, and he didn't hesitate to answer. "Aye. I didn't think it possible after Caitlin…but I see now that wasn't love at all. A dream. An obsession. I've never known a woman with a truer heart than Nora—by God, Ronan, I will not lose her!"

He lunged in fury from the chair even as Ronan rose beside him to clasp his shoulder. "You will not lose her, Niall. We *will* prevail. Now go home! The woman you love awaits you there."

Niall was already striding for the door while Ronan came behind him.

Aye, they both had women they loved more than life waiting for them at home!

CHAPTER 14

It wasn't the whisper of her name at her ear that woke Nora, but the tender kiss at her temple that made her open her eyes.

"Niall…" So glad to see him, she flung her arms around his neck as he found her mouth to kiss her with an intensity that took her breath away.

She kissed him back with equal measure, so thankful he was home, so grateful to feel him crushing her against him as if he would never let her go.

Finally he did release her, though, to stand beside the bed while he pulled her up so she was seated facing him. His smile thrilled her heart as his gaze swept her shirt and trousers.

"I leave you with Triona and look what she's done. Made a wild hellion of you just like when she first came to Glenmalure!"

Nora knew he was teasing her and she launched herself

from the bed into his arms, his mouth finding hers again.

She could not say how long they kissed so breathlessly, but she felt lightheaded, her heart pounding when he released her to gaze into her eyes.

"Miss me?"

"Oh, aye, Niall!" She stared back at him, drinking in the sight of his handsome face in the flickering lamplight though he did look tired. The reality behind his fatigue came flooding back to her then, and suddenly stricken, she cast down her eyes. "I'm so sorry, husband. So very sorry about the ring. It once belonged to my sister Kristina...and must have slipped out of the pouch—"

"Shh, wife, don't trouble yourself about it any longer." Niall's forefinger lifted her chin gently so she faced him again. "No one blames you for anything, my love...and certainly not me."

She blinked, gazing into his eyes.

My love.

Her heart suddenly filled with such joy, she had no words to speak.

Niall seemed content with no words between them, too, and drew her into his arms to hug her tightly, his hand cradling the back of her neck and his fingers entwining in her hair.

For long moments she rejoiced in the strong, steady beat of his heart against her ear and his cheek resting atop her head, the two of them simply standing there holding each other.

She felt the rise and fall of his chest at last as he sighed, and she sighed, too, feeling so bereft when he drew back from her. She swore she saw moisture in his eyes and her heart went out to him as she raised her hand to touch his face.

"Niall, all will be well. It *has* to be—oh!"

He had taken her hand in his strong one to bury an impassioned kiss in her palm. She felt him shudder even as she trembled…and then she was standing no more as he picked her up and laid her on the bed.

He straightened, and she saw his hands shaking as he swiftly stripped himself of his sword belt and clothing, his eyes never leaving hers. It seemed within a moment he was naked and he joined her on the bed, the mattress shifting beneath his weight as he straddled her knees.

He bent over her, his hands working fast to untie the leather cord at her waist and pull the trousers from her hips, her thighs, and then tug them from her feet and toss them to the floor. Still his eyes never left hers while she could but stare at him, her heart racing and her breath frozen in her throat.

Yet she gasped when he went next for her shirt and slipped his warm hands underneath her camise to move up along her trembling belly, her ribs, her breasts to pull the two garments quickly over her head.

Then she was naked, too, shivering beneath him as his gaze swept her, intense, hungry.

"Woman, you are so beautiful to me. So beautiful…"

Her throat closed with emotion, she could only watch as he raised himself above her to find her lips once more…kissing her so wildly, almost desperately that her heart raced even faster. Yet before she could reach up to tunnel her fingers in his hair, his mouth had moved to her throat, trailing heated kisses.

Then to her breastbone, his hands covering her breasts to caress her there while his mouth found a swollen nipple to suckle hungrily.

She closed her eyes and threw back her head, arching beneath him, but nothing prepared her for when he suddenly trailed his tongue down her abdomen to dip into her navel.

He seemed intent upon kissing every inch of her, but when he moved even lower to the dusky woman's hair at the heart of her thighs, she felt she could no longer breathe.

Yet she was breathing, harder, faster, when he spread her legs and lowered himself between them to press his mouth there, spearing his tongue into her.

She cried out as his mouth claimed her, her slick folds made only wetter as he suckled and teased the swollen nub she felt pulsing, throbbing, from his lips, his tongue.

Her head thrown back, she tried to close her thighs but he held her fast. His hands cupped her bottom to draw her closer so he might delve his tongue into her that much deeper.

Her body began to shake, her fingers twisting in the linen sheets. Suddenly, Niall raised himself over her again to balance himself upon one arm and guide his swollen shaft to the place where his mouth had been.

She glanced down at the moment the silken tip of his flesh rubbed against her, the warm, slippery wetness of his shaft melding with hers as he slowly, oh so slowly, began to thrust himself into her.

She watched him, trembling, mesmerized, as his thick hard length disappeared within her body, and then withdrew again, Niall's breath coming harder, the muscles bulging in the arm supporting him.

Only when he guided himself into her once more, his thumb flicking at the quivering nub now on fire from the slow onslaught of his flesh rubbing against her, did Nora throw back her head to scream.

Yet she heard nothing, his ragged groan filling her mouth and silencing her as his powerful body came down upon hers, his thrusting hips catapulting her to a place she'd never been to before.

Did she hear him cry out her name? That was her last conscious thought as her climax exploded over her. Wildly she clutched at his shoulders, her trembling legs bracing against his hard buttocks.

Distantly she felt him drive himself into her and he was then shuddering, too, the fierce throbbing of his flesh making her scream into his mouth when a second climax gripped her.

Oh God, oh God, oh God...

Nora could not say at what moment she no longer lay beneath Niall but atop him as he rolled with her to the opposite side of the bed.

Breathless, satiated, she could only collapse upon him

as his arms flew around her to hug her against his sweat-slicked chest...once more his heartbeat thudding fast and strong and steady in her ear.

"I love you, Nora O'Byrne. Love you..."

Tears welling behind her closed eyes to hear the words she'd so longed for, Nora breathed brokenly, "I love you, Niall O'Byrne. My husband...my heart..."

They must have dozed, even slept for a while...Nora oblivious to the passage of time until she fluttered open her eyes to find that Niall was no longer in the bed with her. Where...?

Sharply drawing in her breath, she sat up only to spy him at the basin across the room splashing water upon his face as if to revive himself.

"Niall?"

He dried himself with a towel and then strode around the bed to her, pulling her into his arms to kiss her fiercely. Yet his embrace was all too brief, his expression somber as he drew back from her.

"I must go. It's my turn with my clansmen at the gates."

"Ah, Niall, please take care! If anything should happen to you—"

"All will be well, remember? It *has* to be." He gathered her hands in his to kiss her fingers. "You must go back to sleep, wife. I'll return before morning."

He left her so abruptly...as if forcing himself from her side, that her hands fell to her lap. She watched as he went to the other side of the bed to gather up his clothing and dress, his face grown all the more grim in the lamplight as he drew on his boots.

Only when he had begun to fasten his sword belt around his waist did they hear a sudden loud pounding on the door of their dwelling-house. Drawing his sword, Niall gestured for her to remain in bed and then ran from the room.

Her heart in her throat, Nora heard him throw open the door to one of his clansmen shouting, "Riders, Niall, approaching the gates!"

Oh, God, no! Already Sigurd and his men were attacking the stronghold? She could no more stay in bed than she could calm the rampant beating of her heart. She flung aside the blankets and jumped out to retrieve her shirt and trousers, the nearest thing at hand.

Niall must have left the door yawning open for she heard men shouting and a terrible commotion, and the thunderous pounding of horses' hooves. Her hands shook as she dressed quickly, but took no time to pull on the shoes Triona had lent her and instead ran barefoot into the adjoining room.

Nora didn't stop running until she was out the dwelling-house door, where she came to a dead stop.

The torchlit yard teemed with armed O'Byrne clansmen as they surrounded a group of at least thirty riders atop snorting horses lathered with sweat...not Norseman at all but what she swore must be Irish. As the massive inner gates closed behind them, a formidable-looking man with coppery hair dismounted from a huge roan stallion to stand in front of Ronan and Niall.

"Donal MacMurrough, you're welcome here among us!" she heard Ronan's raised voice greet the man who stood as tall as him, while to Nora's surprise suddenly Triona appeared as if out of nowhere at her side. She wore a white sleeping gown, her hair wild and disheveled as if she'd flown out of bed.

"Nora…"

Triona didn't say more, and Nora could not fathom why her sister-in-law looked so stricken…not like Triona at all.

Yet it was a flash of silky blond hair that drew Nora's gaze back to the cluster of men and horses in front of the gates, a young woman of unsurpassed beauty breaking through the crowd.

"Oh, Niall, I didn't know that you'd even be here! Please forgive me…I beg you to forgive me!"

With arms outflung, the young woman launched herself at Niall and he caught her…while Nora was certain she felt her heart suddenly break.

Caitlin.

CHAPTER 15

Niall was so stunned he didn't know what to say, all words had fled him. He stared in disbelief at Caitlin as she pulled back to look at him, her lovely face flushed bright pink and her emerald eyes alight.

"Oh, Niall, I've asked for weeks for my father to bring me here so I might speak with you and finally he relented! We rode from Ferns all day and even when it grew dark, I pleaded for him not to stop until we reached Glenmalure. We knew from Ronan only that you'd disappeared so I planned to wait with your family as long as it took until you returned—but you're here!"

Again she made to throw her arms around his neck, but Niall stepped back from her, her breathless torrent of words making no sense to him.

Nothing made sense to him except that he'd glanced over his shoulder to see Nora standing in front of their dwelling-house with Triona…Nora looking so deathly pale as if the blood had drained from her face.

"Lord MacMurrough…Caitlin, if you'll give me a

moment so I might fetch my wife."

"Y-your wife?" Her mouth dropped open, now it was Caitlin who appeared wholly stunned as she glanced from her now somber-faced father to Niall, who left them to stride toward Nora.

Her gaze never left his face as he drew closer, and he could see at once from the rapid rise and fall of her breasts that she was finding it difficult to catch her breath. She looked so dumbstruck that he wanted nothing more than to crush her within his arms to reassure her, but that would have to wait.

Triona appeared so taken aback as well that Niall could only imagine what she must be thinking. He held out his hand to Nora, not surprised to see how visibly she was shaking.

In the next instant she looked horrified, too, as she glanced down at her clothing, and her bare feet, though she took his hand with trembling fingers. Niall said nothing but walked swiftly with her back to Caitlin, Donal MacMurrough, and their silent entourage, where he stopped and drew Nora against him, still clasping her hand.

"Caitlin…Lord MacMurrough, if I may present my wife, Nora O'Byrne."

Nora looked at Caitlin and Caitlin blinked at Nora, the beautiful blonde's green eyes welling with tears. No one said a word, the stronghold yard eerily silent but for the neighing of horses, crackling torches, and the awkward shuffling of feet as lightning streaked above them across the night sky.

If not for a sudden clap of thunder that made everyone jump, Nora was certain they would all still be there staring uncomfortably at each other. Another brilliant flash of lightning followed by a second deafening clap sent everyone into motion, Ronan raising his voice in command.

"Clansmen to your posts! Niall, it's your watch! Donal, we face imminent attack on the morrow. You're welcome to remain here for the night, but it's best you ride home now to Ferns—"

"Too late, Ronan," the chieftain said, gesturing for the rest of his men to dismount from their horses. "As we rode to the gates, I spied movement against the hill. I thought mayhap some clan with a grudge against you...but apparently it's far worse. I fear your enemy is here...or advance scouts at the very least."

A terrible sinking feeling gripped Nora as Niall turned to her, still clasping her hand. He looked so grim, his intense gaze holding hers.

"Your trust is all I need right now, Nora. Go back to our home where I know you're safe."

She nodded while Caitlin still stared at them, tears streaking the young woman's pale cheeks, her soft sobs filling Nora with pity.

As Niall released her hand to stride away, thunder crashed above them and jagged lightning lit up the dark sky. The next thing Nora knew Triona stood by her side as if to accompany her back to her dwelling-house, but she shook her head no.

"Look after Caitlin. I'll be all right."

Nora didn't feel all right, but somehow she summoned the strength to move as Triona went to Caitlin. O'Byrne clansmen rushed forward to lead skittish horses to the stables while Donal MacMurrough ordered his own men to gather around him.

"Aye, Donal, you and your men follow me to the feasting-hall and I'll tell you all!" Ronan shouted as the sky suddenly opened up in a fierce torrent of rain.

Nora was soaked to the skin by the time she reached the dwelling-house, but her wooden legs had prevented her from walking any faster.

She felt numb. With rain-chilled fingers she went inside and closed the door behind her...and this time she did collapse to the floor.

In the firelight, Ronan grimly faced men who had long been enemies of the O'Byrnes until two years' past, the night unprecedented to have MacMurroughs within his stronghold and under his roof. Yet the moment he'd seen Caitlin among them as they rode through the gates, he had known this night would be unlike any other.

What could be said, though? Everyone knew that Caitlin had spurned Niall...and now Niall had wed another, no matter under what circumstances. Ronan thought of Nora, pitying her, but then he forced away the image of her eyes widened with disbelief at seeing Caitlin rush into Niall's arms.

Damn it all, was it not enough that Sigurd Knutson's

men were already at their doorstep? The rest of his Norsemen and Magnus MacTorkil's Ostmen soon to descend upon them? If the torrential rain continued, it might buy them another day or two but the threat of battle still loomed.

Cursing vehemently under his breath, Ronan met Donal's somber gaze as one of the most powerful chieftains in all of Éire and close ally of the Normans leaned forward to press him.

"I urge you again, Ronan, send word to your brother-in-law Duncan FitzWilliam! He has heavy horse and armored knights! One look at such a force and Sigurd Knutson will think better of this folly and march straight back to Ostmentown, four hundred men or no!"

"*I will not!*" Ronan's roar echoed from the rafters, but Donal didn't flinch or sit back in his chair. Instead he rose to stare fiercely down at him.

"Like it or not, Ronan O'Byrne, Lord FitzWilliam is blood to you now that he's taken Maire to wife. Family! Just as *I* am family to you through my niece Triona, though God knows, I would never have imagined such a thing was possible two years ago. You cannot do else but send word to him! Your clansmen are outnumbered! *We're* outnumbered for I'm here with you now, aye, and my men and beloved daughter as well. Will your stubborn pride threaten us all?"

Ronan clenched his jaw and looked away, his silence making Donal swear now, too, and turn in frustration to the freshly stoked fire in the massive hearth.

Irish and Norman! The words echoing in his mind, his heart, Ronan clenched his fists as Triona's lovely face appeared to him, Deirdre's face, Maire's face, Niall's face, and Nora's, too.

If he bent this far and sent word to Longford Castle in Meath as Donal wished him to do, would it make him break? Or mayhap might he be strong enough to turn his back upon everything he'd fought for, everything he believed in...if only to protect the lives of the people he loved?

"Aye, Donal, send two of your men to your stronghold in Ferns and I'll send two of mine to Duncan FitzWilliam. We can spare no more. God help us that reinforcements reach us in time!"

"Ah, Nora, no..." Triona whisked off her sodden cloak just inside the door, the rain still a driving deluge. She knelt down in her sleeping gown next to her sister-in-law who lay as if unconscious on the floor. "Nora, do you hear me?"

The small nod swamped Triona with relief, though her concern was great that Nora looked so pale, her lips tinged with blue. No wonder with her wet clothes plastered to her body!

Triona regretted now that she hadn't come sooner. She cursed under her breath that Caitlin's noisy sobbing over Niall and desperate pleading that Triona remain by her side had kept her from the one that needed her most.

"Nora, let me help you to bed. We need to get you

warm!" Relief swept Triona again that Nora had the strength to sit up and drape her arm around Triona's shoulders, and then struggle to her feet.

Together they made their way to the adjoining room, Nora not saying a word though she managed a small, grateful smile. As soon as they neared the bed, Triona stopped her and without blinking an eye, helped her to strip out of her wet clothes.

"Aye, now, sit down on the edge of the bed while I fetch you a sleeping gown." As Nora, shivering from head to toe, obliged her, Triona flew to a heavy wooden chest across the room and threw open the lid. She was so glad to return and help Nora into the sleeping gown, and then settle her into bed and draw blankets up to her chin.

Triona didn't stop there, but hurried back into the main room and stoked the hearth fire until the flames crackled. Already the place felt warmer and soon the bedchamber would, too. Then she spied the cups of ale on the table, both barely touched.

Aye, something bracing! She grabbed one, took a sip herself, and then hurried back to Nora. She wasn't surprised to see her sister-in-law's stunning blue eyes welling with tears, one trickling down her cheek.

Clucking her tongue as her beloved maid Aud used to do, Triona slipped her arm underneath Nora's head and brought the cup to her pale lips. "Go on, Nora, take a good swallow. It will revive you, I promise!"

Thankfully Nora did as Triona bade her, though so big a gulp that Nora began to cough and sputter. Triona started to laugh, more out of further relief than humor, she felt so heartened to see Nora's face flushed a healthy pink.

"Aye, drink up 'til it's gone, Nora O'Byrne, and no more tears. I'll admit it's been a surprising night, but can you not take heart at how quickly Niall claimed you as his wife?"

Nora sputtered again, wiping the ale from her chin, and nodded.

"Good! I was beginning to think when I found you upon the floor that you'd not noticed. Niall loves you. You love him. It's been plain for all of us to see. Have some faith in your husband, Nora! Did you not hear him ask you to trust him?"

"Aye, I did," Nora said softly, handing Triona the empty cup. "How is Caitlin?"

Triona sighed heavily, shaking her head. "As self-centered it appears as her heart is fickle. I don't know that she's even considered how things must appear to you, though here you're asking after her welfare. Aye, Maire would have done the same thing, the two of you cut from a more compassionate cloth than most, truly."

"So Caitlin did not marry?"

"Apparently not, the MacMurrough's godson Brian suffering the same fate as Niall—and hopefully he'll find a lovely true-hearted bride to wed as well!" Triona leaned forward to tuck the blankets more securely around Nora's shoulders. "I love my cousin, but I pity my poor uncle, too. To have catered to her whim that they ride here so she might wait for Niall—well, at least now we've a chance others might come to help us."

"Help?"

Nora's eyes grown wide, Triona nodded. "Riders left the stronghold as I ran to your house. God help them that the rain grants them cover out of Glenmalure. Ronan sent me word while I was tending to Caitlin that two men are bound for Ferns and two to Maire's Duncan in Meath. I never thought I'd see the day when Ronan might ask for aid from a Norman…aye, no matter his own brother now by marriage…"

Now Triona felt tears burn her eyes, Nora reaching out to squeeze her hand. Triona gave a small laugh, and squeezed her hand back. "You're a wonder, Nora O'Byrne. So kind and caring. Niall is a fortunate man to have found you!"

Teary smiles between both of them now, Triona settled herself on the edge of the bed. "I'll stay with you a while longer, but you must try to sleep."

Nora nodded, and once more she squeezed Triona's hand. "Thank you, Triona…for everything."

"Jesu, Mary, and Joseph, no thanks are needed! We're sisters, you and I…and we O'Byrnes stand together!"

Deep in the night and long after Triona had left her side, Nora awakened to the mattress giving way beneath Niall's weight as he climbed naked into bed and drew her against him.

She knew how exhausted he must be when he fell

asleep within moments, his chin nuzzled against her shoulder and his breathing low and steady.

Lying there with his muscular arms around her, Nora remembered how intensely he had stared at her earlier that night, his fervent words burning in her mind…

Your trust is all I need right now, Nora.

Aye, she had never ceased to trust him…though with Caitlin here and still so infatuated with him and her angelic blond beauty beyond compare—

"No, you will not think of it!" Nora chided herself, closing her eyes and snuggling closer to her sleeping husband.

All would be well between her and Niall. It *had* to be!

CHAPTER 16

"It's only because I need you to seek an annulment from Rome that I've let you live, MacTorkil," Sigurd grated as he glared at the ashen-faced merchant seated atop a horse next to him. "It galls me still that you thought I wouldn't notice you'd sent one of your men to warn the O'Byrnes. Look now as the mist rises with the sun! The bastards don't even know yet that my full forces are here!"

Sigurd followed Magnus's gaze not to the O'Byrne stronghold appearing through the dense fog that shrouded Glenmalure, but to the captured MacMurrough clansman lying beaten and unconscious upon the ground in front of them.

"Fools! Three others eluded my scouts last night but this one told them enough once they persuaded him to loosen his tongue. Let Ronan O'Byrne and Donal MacMurrough cling to their delusion a few moments more that any help will come soon enough to save them!"

Sigurd signaled for several of his Norsemen to pick up

their prisoner and throw his limp body over a horse. The rest of his men and Magnus's Ostmen stood ready and silent behind him to march from their elevated position to the opposite end of Glenmalure.

Shields raised.

Scores of tall ladders constructed to breach the stronghold's two outer ramparts and inner palisade.

His men muddy and soaked to the skin from the rainy trek in the dark from Glendalough, but by Odin, what did they care? They had sailed from a land of fjords and mist and thunder and exulted in such weather!

Just as Sigurd exulted now...so close to reclaiming his bride that he could already feel her naked body writhing beneath him as he buried himself to the hilt inside her. Hear her moans, her pleas for him to stop, her screams!

She would pay for humiliating him by fleeing the night before their wedding—by all the gods in Valhalla, she would pay.

Grinding his teeth, Sigurd could contain his impatience no longer, nor his fury.

As the sun broke through the low clouds to burn away still more of the morning fog, he dug his heels into the massive black steed beneath him and signaled for his men to begin their march.

"Niall! By God, Niall, wake up!"

Stunned to find Ronan standing beside the bed with his sword in hand, Niall sat up as Nora gasped beside him.

"Ronan...what?"

"Sigurd Knutson and his Norsemen are marching across the glen toward us! Flann O'Faelin spied them from his post as the fog lifted and sounded the alarm!"

Niall vaulted from the bed to retrieve his clothes, Ronan already charging from the room. Nora looked wide-eyed with fright, the blankets clutched to her chin.

"You must get dressed and go to the feasting-hall," he bade her grimly as he donned his clothing and boots. "All the women and children will be gathering there—and stay close to Triona. We've arrows aplenty to fend off an attack, but our enemy has greater numbers. If the word comes from Ronan, Triona will know what to do."

"Do?"

Niall nodded as he fastened his sword belt around his waist, wishing he'd had a chance to prepare Nora more for what might come. "Aye, an escape route in the kitchen. A trap door in the larder leading to a tunnel. If the stronghold is breached, as many women and children as can make it there must attempt to flee into the hills—"

"Oh, Niall!"

He came around the bed to meet her as she flew to him, nearly tripping on her sleeping gown. He crushed her in his arms, not surprised she was shaking. Yet he couldn't linger, no matter how much he ached to.

No matter how much he had hoped to awaken her with a kiss and hold her close and make love to her and reassure her that she alone, held his heart.

Reluctantly, he pulled back from her to stare into her

eyes, though he hadn't found the will yet to fully release her. "Nora, I must go. Heed me and get dressed. There's no time to waste."

She nodded, her trembling fingers reaching up to caress the side of his face, his lips. So softly she murmured, "I love you," and Niall felt his throat grow tight.

"I love you, Nora O'Byrne. Nothing has changed between us. *Nothing.*"

He bent his head to kiss her and she clung to him, while he embraced her fiercely again for one more precious moment. Then he forced himself to release her though her arms still reached for him…his last image of her as he lunged out the door.

Duncan FitzWilliam closed his eyes against the first rays of sunlight streaming through the narrow arched windows, and tightened his embrace around his sleeping wife.

Maire O'Byrne FitzWilliam…his beautiful bride of one week though it felt like only moments ago that they had arrived at Longford Castle and he had roared for a priest to be fetched from the parish church to wed them.

Duncan had vowed that day never to forget that she was an O'Byrne first before a FitzWilliam, for she had given up so much to become his wife.

Her home in Glenmalure. Her family. Everything.

Duncan sighed heavily, abandoning any notion of trying to sleep just a while longer.

He was wide awake now while Maire still slept peacefully, her long midnight hair fanning out behind her like a lustrous veil upon the pillow.

He could not forget, either, the hatred in Ronan O'Byrne's eyes as they had clashed with swords outside the O'Byrne stronghold a week ago when Duncan had gone to claim Maire as his bride. Two months earlier Ronan had saved his life but this time, he had struck blows intended to kill Duncan until Ronan's courageous wife Triona had rushed into the fray to stop them.

Ronan despised Normans, Duncan included, for which he could not blame him.

Invading Normans had seized O'Byrne lands in Kildare, burned their homes, and forced them to take refuge in the Wicklow Mountains.

Invading Normans had pillaged, raped, and slaughtered their way across Leinster and left festering resentment and rage in their wake.

Most of those clans had nonetheless accepted the yoke of foreign rule, including the MacMurroughs whose own Dermot, King of Leinster, had invited the Normans to Ireland forty years past to help him regain his kingdom from rival chieftains. Yet rebel clans like the O'Byrnes and O'Tooles had never bowed to the invaders, and instead were bent upon driving the Normans out by raiding against them.

By the blood of God, Duncan would allow no one to harry him from the lands King John had granted him, yet he craved peace, too!

Especially now. His battle-scarred hand tender as he caressed Maire's shoulder, Duncan thought again of Ronan and wished things could be different...if only for her.

He knew how much she loved her family though she had left them to follow her heart...and for that Duncan would be forever grateful.

"Duncan?"

Maire's sweet voice like balm to his troubled musing, Duncan gazed into the lovely face of the woman he loved more than life.

She looked up at him drowsily, still satiated from their lovemaking that had carried them well into the night. "You cannot sleep?"

He drew her close and kissed her forehead, the tip of her nose, and last her lips that parted beneath his, her breath catching as he swept his tongue into her mouth.

After being separated from her for those two agonizing months when he had healed from his grievous wound and then sailed to England to seek permission from King John to wed her, he could not get his fill of her. He never would!

Already he was hard for her, painfully so. He eased her onto her back to gaze down into her smiling gray eyes.

"You tease me, woman. It's not sleep you're thinking of."

She laughed softly, and lifted her hand to caress his face. "Aye, you've read me well, husband. I don't wish to fault you...but I believe there's a place you neglected to kiss last night—oh!"

Her delighted cry drowned out by his lusty roar, she

was soon giggling as he threw aside the blankets and then raised himself to his hands and knees above her.

"Hmmm, did you mean here?" He lowered his head to press a burning kiss to her navel while she sucked in her breath, her giggling ceased. "Or mayhap here?"

He began to trail kisses down her trembling abdomen, the tempting midnight triangle at the apex of her thighs beckoning to him—

"Lord FitzWilliam, forgive me, but I must speak to you at once! Lord FitzWilliam!"

Cursing at the anxious voice of one of his knights outside their bedchamber, followed by fierce pounding, Duncan vaulted from the bed as Maire gathered the blankets to cover herself. He didn't bother to pull on his braies, but threw open the door.

"God's teeth, man, what is it?"

"Two O'Byrne clansmen from Glenmalure, my lord, bearing an urgent message from their chieftain Black O'Byrne and Donal MacMurrough. They face imminent attack and ask for your help!"

"My brother?"

Duncan didn't have to glance at Maire to know that she stared at him in shock. Already he was thrusting one leg and then the other into his braies, and then he lunged past his grim-faced knight to descend the tower steps two at a time.

Maire had never seen such a show of force as what had

assembled so quickly in the bailey, and she felt both awed and terrified.

Fifty armored knights atop heavy horse, their chain mail glinting in the sunlight, and twice as many mounted men-at-arms bearing crossbows awaited Duncan's signal as he mounted his powerful bay stallion.

His farewell kiss still burned upon Maire's lips and she could not tear her eyes from him as he sought her gaze, too. A glance of such fierce love flew between them that she felt her heart race even faster.

Duncan FitzWilliam, Baron of Longford, had answered her brother's call. *He had answered her brother's call!*

So overcome that her husband would be willing to risk life and limb to aid Ronan and her clansmen, Maire felt grateful tears burn her eyes even as fear gripped her for Duncan's safety.

Would he return home to her safe and whole? More frightening questions assailed her as he tore his gaze from her and gave the signal for his men to ride with him from the fortress.

Might the Norsemen's attack have already begun? Would Duncan and his men arrive at Glenmalure in time to save her family? Ronan and Triona and little Deirdre…and Niall and his new bride, Nora—*his new bride!*

Maire couldn't have been more astounded to hear from Duncan as he dressed for battle what the two exhausted O'Byrne clansmen had relayed to him about Niall's marriage. Yet any joy she had felt for her beloved brother had been overshadowed at once by their dire circumstances.

Caitlin and her father Donal MacMurrough and their clansmen were in grave peril, too—dear God, protect them all!

Maire wanted so desperately to catch a last glimpse of her husband as he and his men thundered across the drawbridge, but with her awkward gait he was beyond her view by the time she was halfway to the gatehouse.

"Oh, Duncan..." Fresh tears bit her eyes though she would not allow herself to cry.

She was mistress of Longford now, and Duncan's people looked to her for courage and resilience in such times of trial.

Bravely she lifted her chin and nodded for the mailed guards that remained behind to protect Longford Castle to raise the massive drawbridge.

CHAPTER 17

"Where is the thief that stole my promised bride?"

Sigurd's roar echoing around him, he cursed as a tall Irishman with dark brown hair appeared on the parapet atop the massive rampart to stand beside who he'd guessed were Ronan O'Byrne and Donal MacMurrough.

With his forces amassed far enough away so the O'Byrnes' arrows wouldn't reach them, Sigurd brandished his broad axe at the three men.

"You have a choice to make, Niall O'Byrne! Give up Nora to me and live to see another day, or we will slaughter all of you!"

Again his thundered words echoed from surrounding hills, Sigurd's rage mounting when no answer came…until a torrent of arrows from the stronghold were suddenly unleashed upon them.

Sigurd didn't flinch, knowing the barrage of deadly missiles would fall short, but the blatant message behind them was clear.

Incensed now, he signaled for his men to bring forth their prisoner, the MacMurrough clansman still unconscious, but no matter. Sigurd knew well enough how to summon a death scream even from men more dead than alive, which had earned him the name *Skullcrusher*.

He dismounted from his snorting steed while Magnus MacTorkil remained as ashen-faced and silent atop his mount not far from him. Sigurd hacked up a ball of phlegm in disgust.

"Damned useless merchant." Striding over to where his men had dumped the prisoner's limp body upon the ground, Sigurd spat upon him and then kicked him in the stomach. He was rewarded by a low groan, which made Sigurd drop to one knee and drive the blade of his axe into the ground.

"You dare to defy me, O'Byrnes?" he bellowed in fury, grabbing the prisoner by the sides of his head and hauling him up in front of him. "Donal MacMurrough, do you recognize this man? He was bound for Ferns to summon your clansmen, but now he's bound for hell!"

Again silence greeted him, though Sigurd could see the faces of his enemy grown even grimmer. With a wild howl, he squeezed the prisoner's head so fiercely that the man screamed in agony—but only for an instant before a distinct crack of bone shattering could be heard and Sigurd dropped the lifeless man to the ground.

His men lined up in rows behind him howled now, too, and beat their weapons upon their shields. The thunderous sound only fueled Sigurd's battle lust as he retrieved his axe and rose to his feet.

"Shield wall!"

In unison his forces lifted their shields to abut each other and began to march forward shoulder to shoulder, while Sigurd merged into the line to join them.

Nora stood stock-still outside the feasting-hall, her heart in her throat.

Triona had sent her out to look for Caitlin, who hadn't yet joined the women and children gathered inside. So many of them were weeping, terrified, that Triona had asked Nora to go so she might stay and comfort her clanswomen as best she could.

Triona had said for Nora to try her and Ronan's dwelling-house, where Caitlin had spent the night, but Nora hadn't made it very far. Instead she had heard the terrible ultimatum Sigurd had roared out to Niall, and had seen the O'Byrnes and MacMurroughs lining the parapets unleash a barrage of deadly arrows in answer.

Dear God, so many willing to die to protect her? So many others crying and frightened in the feasting-hall, not knowing what was to come? Women fearing for their husbands and tearful children calling out for their fathers— God help her, it was too much to bear!

Her back pressed against the timbered wall, Nora had heard the stomach-turning crack of bone, too, in the ominous silence after Sigurd had baited Donal MacMurrough about capturing one of his clansmen. Now that poor man was dead because of her! Her presence here had brought this unspeakable horror down upon Ronan and Triona and their people, aye, and especially Niall!

If Sigurd and his Norsemen managed to breach the stronghold's defenses, who would that monster run looking for with his broad axe raised high but her husband?

Sickened and more terrified than she had ever felt in her life, Nora heard the wild battle cries of Sigurd's forces drawing closer and knew she must find Caitlin. She didn't want to risk Triona sending out anyone else to look for her, or mayhap even Triona leaving the feasting-hall to search now for both of them.

Somehow Nora made herself move. She lifted her blue silk gown and ran toward Ronan and Triona's dwelling-house…until a sudden glimpse of blond hair made her stop and look toward the parapet abutting the massive inner gate.

She saw Ronan and Niall there…saw Niall turn around as if startled, and then Caitlin rushed toward him to fling herself in his arms.

To press her lips to Niall's as he gathered her close, one hand still gripping his sword. Together, they ducked down along with Ronan when a slew of arrows went whizzing above their heads.

"Oh, God, Niall, no…" Nora heard thunks all around her as arrows struck the walls behind her, the roofs above her, and the ground beside her. Yet she scarcely noticed, instead meeting Niall's gaze across the distance separating them when he suddenly spied her.

It seemed for an instant that time stood still...Nora not breathing, her heart thundering in her ears, and then she began to run.

Not for the feasting-hall, but the kitchen next door.

Tears threatening to blind her, she didn't stop even when she'd entered the low building but ran straight for the larder.

No one stopped her. No one was there. Everyone either preparing to fight or taking refuge in the feasting-hall from the terror descending upon them.

God in heaven, because of *her*! Doing her best to block out the image of Niall embracing Caitlin from her mind, Nora choked back sobs and ducked into the larder and wildly looked for the trap door.

A steel ring caught her eye and she rushed forward to grasp the cold metal to lift the door and drop it with a bang to the floor. The yawning darkness of the tunnel below her, it was only then that she saw a row of flickering lamps upon a nearby table as if prepared and waiting for scores of weeping women and children.

Yet there was no one else to grab one of the lanterns and clamber down into the musty-smelling tunnel other than Nora.

Tears streaking her face, she held up the lantern to light the way and ran forward into the darkness, the ceiling buttressed with timber high enough so she didn't have to duck her head. Her breath coming in gasps, she had no idea how far she'd gone along the tunnel when she spied a ladder ahead and knew she'd come to the end.

Nothing made sense to her any longer but that she had to stop the terror, stop the attack. Her knees shaking, she dropped the lantern and scaled the ladder, dirt raining down upon her when she pushed open the wooden door.

The brilliant sunlight blinded her as she climbed out, but she didn't stop. Sweeping up her gown above her knees, she ran down the hill toward a terrifying phalanx of raised shields moving en masse toward the stronghold.

She spied her father further back from the melee atop a horse that tossed its head at the deafening commotion, but she didn't run toward him. Instead she made straight for the chilling apparition of a giant towering above all the rest behind his massive shield, screaming his name.

"Sigurd!"

God in heaven, how would he hear her above the howls of his men? Yet as if she were an apparition herself upon the field of battle, Norsemen and Ostmen alike began to stop in their tracks and stare at her as if they couldn't believe their eyes.

Falling silent one by one and then by dozens, until she saw Sigurd turn his shaven, tattooed head in her direction…and raise his broad axe high.

"By Odin, cease!"

All at once everything around Nora fell silent but for her rasping effort to draw breath and her heartbeat roaring in her ears.

Out of the corner of her eye she spied him then, Niall climbing atop the parapet with Ronan and Donal MacMurrough grabbing his arms as if to prevent him from jumping the twenty feet to the ground.

"*Nora!*"

His cry agonized, she caught a glimpse of his stricken face just as Sigurd reached her to grab a fistful of her hair and yank her against him.

"Foolish bitch!" he roared at her, digging his fingers into her scalp. "What good are you to me if you'd been killed?"

"I am here! Is that not enough?" Staring up into his face mottled with rage, she heard her ragged voice begging him, pleading with him. "Please stop the attack! If there is a way, I will be your wife!"

"Have no doubt you'll become my bride as soon as an annulment is granted for your heinous marriage to that bastard O'Byrne! I'll not stop until he feels the blade of my axe buried in his skull!"

"No…" Nora's legs gave way beneath her, but Sigurd dragged her by the hair to the closest of his men and thrust her at them.

"Take her from the field and renew the attack! Shield wall!"

A resounding roar went up as Sigurd's forces obeyed his command, but it was the driving pounding of hooves toward them that made Nora turn her head.

"You have my daughter, Sigurd!" Magnus MacTorkil's enraged voice rose above the din as he reined in his horse in front of the huge Norseman. "By God, I swear you'll have neither the gold nor your annulment from Rome if you and your forces don't depart from Glenmalure this very hour!"

Nora feared her father might be struck dead at that moment for how fiercely Sigurd glared at him, but then a twisted smile lit his broad pox-marked face.

"True, MacTorkil, I have your daughter. For now, as she said, it is enough...but not for long."

As Magnus dismounted to rush toward Nora, Sigurd spun around to brandish his axe at the stronghold.

"So you will live another day after all, Niall O'Byrne! Mayhap the daughter of Donal MacMurrough will yet spread her legs as your bride, what do you say?"

Sigurd's coarse laughter ringing out across the glen was the thing Nora heard as she collapsed into darkness in her father's arms.

CHAPTER 18

"Niall, set aside your rage and *think*! You cannot hope to try and wrest Nora from Sigurd in broad daylight! You must wait until dark as when we raid. O'Byrne strength lies not in numbers but in stealth!"

Ronan's hand gripping his arm, Niall cursed as he glanced past his brother into the distance at the last of Sigurd Knutson's men marching from the glen.

Nora was with them. *The woman he loved was with them*!

Again Niall tried to break free from Ronan, but his brother held him fast while their huge clansman, Flann O'Faelin, stood ready to grab him as well. All he'd been able to do was watch helplessly—impotently!—from the parapet as Nora was taken from him by the biggest, ugliest beast of a man that Niall had ever seen.

Aye, Sigurd Knutson was a monster, just as Nora had named him. A monster atop a huge steed who had ridden away with Nora limp and unconscious in his arms!

Sigurd's forces had left nothing behind them but the trampled body of the man Sigurd had brutally slain with his bare hands. Only moments ago had Ronan deemed their enemy far enough away so the gates could be thrown open for the MacMurroughs to retrieve their fallen clansman.

To ride home as well to Ferns if Donal MacMurrough had so decided, but instead the chieftain had said grimly that they would stay and abide by whatever plan Ronan devised to go after Nora.

He'd added, too, that Clan MacMurrough would not stand for Sigurd Knutson and his Norsemen and Magnus MacTorkil's Ostmen to be tramping about Leinster. Without it being said, both Niall and Ronan knew that the Normans would not allow such a show of force to go unchallenged, either. Though it galled Niall, more was at stake than regaining his wife... *if* they were able to overtake Sigurd and his men before reaching their ships in Ostmentown.

"Very well, Ronan," Niall spat out, not calmer at all but forcing himself to think more clearly. As enraged at himself to have caused Nora such pain, however unintended, that she would flee from the stronghold through their escape tunnel, he met his brother's eyes. "What is our plan?"

"We ride within the hour. Keep to the hills and out of sight. After their trek here and now on their way north again, they'll need to rest and likely camp in Glendalough for the night—"

"*Damn him!*" Again Niall strained against Ronan, who still hadn't released his arm.

He didn't want to think about the night!

He didn't want to think about what Sigurd might do to

Nora even before he gained an annulment from Rome!

Aye, Niall had heard it all from the parapet as Magnus MacTorkil had confronted Sigurd, nor was it lost upon Niall that his kind-hearted wife might have sacrificed herself to spare the people she loved from an attack. God help him, if Sigurd so much as touched her…!

"Release me, Ronan! There is something I must do before we ride. Caitlin…" Niall didn't say more, but understanding flew between him and Ronan, who dropped his hand from Niall's arm and let him pass by.

It had been Ronan who had signaled to Niall that Caitlin was behind him on the parapet atop the palisade, Niall turning around just as Caitlin lunged forward to throw herself into his arms.

He and Ronan had rushed to the inner parapet to direct the battle after Sigurd and his men had raised a shield wall to begin the attack, and Caitlin must have seen Niall there and climbed the steps to reach him.

To kiss him when he had pulled her close to keep her from tumbling off the edge of the parapet, and then all three of them ducking to evade the enemy's arrows.

Niall had followed their deadly arc into the stronghold yard and then he'd seen Nora staring up at him as arrows landed all around her.

That alone had sent his heart pounding to his throat…but the look of disbelief on her face to see Caitlin in his arms had nearly felled him. Then Nora had begun to run at the same moment Donal MacMurrough had reached them to take his daughter in hand, while Niall believed

Nora had fled to the feasting-hall.

He had thought her safe from any more arrows and with Triona...until like a horrific nightmare unfolding in front of him, their attackers had ceased their battle cries and he'd heard Nora's voice screaming for Sigurd.

Not from inside the stronghold but beyond the outer rampart. In shock Niall had rushed there only to see the hulking giant seize her by the hair—

"No more!" Niall grated to himself, trying to shut out that terrible image from his mind as he made his way along two narrow wooden bridges connecting the parapets.

Yet he knew he could not shut it out even as he knew if Ronan and Donal MacMurrough hadn't stopped him, he would have jumped from that rampart to certain death.

His only thought had been to reach Nora...but as that fiend Sigurd Knutson had taunted him, Niall would indeed live another day to find him and kill him—

"Niall!"

He had barely climbed down from the last parapet into the stronghold yard when Caitlin hastened toward him. Her lovely face pale, her green eyes desperate, she reached out to him but Niall caught her hands to stop her.

Aye, he blamed himself for this misunderstanding most of all.

He should have explained to Caitlin from the very first that there was nothing any longer between them, but he had thought introducing Nora as his wife would quell any such notions. Now he could see from the way Caitlin looked at him that she still believed there might be a chance—

"Oh, Niall, it's terrible what's happened, truly…but mayhap everything has worked out the way it was meant to be! Your marriage will be annulled and then we can be together—"

"No, Caitlin. I'm going after Nora, hopefully to bring her home."

For a moment Caitlin stared at him in utter disbelief, until at last she sputtered, "That…that plain-faced Ostwoman? How could you possibly want her more than me?"

Niall stared back at her, wondering what could have happened to the tenderhearted young woman he had once thought Caitlin to be.

Mayhap her matchless beauty had tainted her somehow and led her to believe that she could do whatever she wanted with no consequence, who could say? In that instant Niall pitied her, but he had no time to be but brutally honest.

"It's a simple thing, Caitlin. Nora has never betrayed me and never would…nor can I live without her. I love my wife with all my heart."

He left Caitlin then staring open-mouthed after him, but his thoughts remained fixed on Nora as he strode to the stables.

Only on Nora.

Nora stared blindly at the walls of the hastily

constructed tent where she lay atop a blanket thrown upon the hard ground.

Her prison in Glendalough for the few hours Sigurd had grudgingly allowed his men to stop and rest before they set out again on their march back to Ostmentown.

No lamp had been given to her, the light outside growing dim as dusk fell over the camp.

A guard stood in front of the tent to deny anyone access but Sigurd…even her father. The last she had glimpsed Magnus was when Sigurd had carried her into the tent and dumped her upon the blanket, and then left cursing his men's fatigue and that they had stopped at all.

Her father had looked so tired, too, more so than Nora had ever seen him. His face haggard and pale, his watery gaze filled with concern as he'd appeared to be fighting to breathe.

That had been several hours ago after a nightmarish ride from Glenmalure clutched in Sigurd's massive arms. His fetid breath had fanned her face, one huge hand upon the reins and the other straying to her breasts more than she wished to recall to squeeze her cruelly.

Yet it had been his coarse whispers in her ear that had chilled her, Sigurd sharing all the lewd things he planned to do to her once the annulment came from Rome and they were wed…if not before.

Rolling onto her side, Nora bit her lip to prevent herself from becoming sick.

She knew her father's threat to withhold the gold he'd promised Sigurd, and his aid in seeking the annulment would only go so far to keep that monster from assaulting her. One day that horrifying moment would come—ah, God!

Unable to breathe now herself, Nora sat up in an effort to calm her racing heart. She must think of something else—*anything!*—but there were few thoughts to cheer her.

At least other than that Sigurd's attack upon the O'Byrnes had been averted...though she could not get Niall's tortured cry out of her head.

Nora!

The agony in his voice echoing over and over in her mind, Nora clasped her fists to her ears as if she could shut out the memory.

He had wanted to jump from the rampart to try to save her, which had told her then how much he must love her. Not Caitlin at all...yet there was nothing to be done about it!

Nora had given herself over to Sigurd, and he would battle any attempt to take her from him. He had told her that when squeezing her breasts and whispering how he would force her down onto her hands and knees...

"No, no, no!" Bile rising in her throat, Nora had to bite her lip harder to keep from vomiting. She came close to screaming with relief when lightning flashed against the tent walls and thunder boomed overhead, so loud and long that the ground seemed to shake.

Aye, a storm would drown out the sound of Niall's voice in her head! She closed her eyes tightly and prayed for wind and rain and more deafening claps of thunder—

"Nora!"

This frantic cry more real than imagined, Nora opened her eyes to find Magnus staggering into the tent, a bloodied knife in his trembling hand.

"Father...?"

"There is no time, Nora, you must run. Flee! The guard is dead...but someone will soon notice..."

His labored voice faltering, he collapsed to his knees. Nora jumped up and rushed to his side to try to help him but he pushed her away.

"No! You must go now! I'm dying, Nora...my heart...this is all I can do to help you. If I know at least that you forgive me for what I've done to you—"

"Oh, Father, I forgive you but please come with me!"

"No, you must run as far away from the camp as you can! Men were seen atop the hills...and even now Sigurd is alerting his forces. If help has come you must try and reach them! Now go!"

With great effort Magnus rose to his feet and lurched to the back of the tent, where he slit the canvas with the knife. Nora could hear commotion building outside, and she rushed to throw her arms around her father's neck.

For a brief moment, Magnus embraced her and then he pushed her toward the opening he'd cut for her. "Please my beloved child, go..."

She did as he bade her, her father crumpling to his knees as Nora ducked outside into a pelting rain, her tears blinding her.

Yet nothing made her wipe them from her eyes faster

than Sigurd's enraged voice bellowing from the opposite end of the tent.

"By the blood of Odin, MacTorkil, you dare to betray me again?"

Nora heard the sounds of a brief struggle, her father's outcry, and then the sickening thunk of Sigurd's axe as his weapon sank into flesh.

"Damn you, Nora, you cannot escape from me!"

"Oh God, oh God!" Her heart slamming in her chest, she wrenched her gown above her knees and began to run even as the storm she'd desperately prayed for erupted in fury above her.

Lightning flaring, thunder crashing, the darkened skies opening up into a driving downpour.

Still she ran wildly as the camp had erupted too, men screaming and scrambling past her as what she swore were arrows whizzed above her head.

And above it all, Sigurd roaring out her name—dear God, coming after her!

CHAPTER 19

Nora had never run so hard and so fast, uphill now as she left the camp behind her, cold rain stinging her eyes.

Was Niall out there somewhere? He must be if Sigurd's forces were under attack! She didn't dare to glance behind her, terrified of what she might see in the flashes of lightning streaking like bony fingers across the sky.

Soaked to the skin now, she gasped for breath and struggled to keep her sodden gown above her knees. She felt the muscles cramping in her legs. She cried out when she stumbled upon loose rocks and nearly fell.

"Oh, God, keep going!" she admonished herself, but nothing spurred her more than Sigurd's violent cursing not too far behind her.

"By Odin, woman, when I catch you...!"

Tasting her tears, Nora knew then that she could not outrun him.

All hope dying, she felt as if everything had grown still inside her, nothing around her feeling real any longer.

Not the deafening claps of thunder.

Not her chilled hands shaking so badly that she could no longer hold up her gown.

Not the harsh breathing drawing closer and closer behind her.

Again she stumbled and this time she fell hard to the ground…while out of the corner of her eye she saw as if in a dream the dark silhouettes of horses charging down the hill.

Atop them riders wielding swords and wearing mail shirts that glinted as lightning flared and Nora felt all strength leave her body, Sigurd's crashing footfalls telling her that he was almost upon her.

She closed her eyes, the side of her face pressed into the cold mud…while as if from afar she heard men shouting, horses snorting, and Sigurd's howling battle cry as she felt him seize her by the hair.

Yet she felt no vicious tug…only something wet and warm that rained down upon her as a dull thud sounded next to her ear.

She heard Sigurd screaming in pain and then a harsh voice coming from someone standing above her…oh, God, Niall's voice.

"Aye, let's see you crush skulls now! Raise your weapon, man, while you've blood left in your body to fight me!"

Nora heard other familiar voices then, Ronan shouting for everyone to stand back to give Niall plenty of room.

Triona crying out Nora's name as she felt herself rolled over, Triona sinking down in the mud to hug her tightly.

Only then did Nora spy the severed arm upon the ground...Sigurd's arm.

Dazed, she looked up to see Niall wielding his sword and circling the Norseman, who brandished his broad axe with his remaining arm.

"You Irish bastard! You stole what was mine—"

"No! You dared to take what was *mine!*"

Lightning glinted off Niall's sword as he lunged with such fury that Sigurd had no chance to swing his axe.

Struck through the heart, the giant Norseman's face contorted in a terrifying grimace as he fell dead before he hit the ground.

The top of his shaven head only inches from Nora's feet, his sightless eyes staring up at her.

She screamed in horror...and in unspeakable relief as Niall rushed toward her to gather her into his arms.

To hold her close and whisper soothing words to her while he strode with her to his horse. He gave her over to Ronan for only a moment while he mounted, and then Nora was lifted up into his arms.

Her cheek pressed to Niall's chest, his heartbeat so strong and reassuring against her ear, Nora watched as Ronan embraced Triona fiercely and then led his wife to her horse as well.

They had both no sooner mounted, other O'Byrne clansmen astride their horses gathered all around them, when a rider approached. Wearing chain mail and seated atop a mighty bay stallion that tossed its great head, the man reined in beside Niall.

"I see the thing is done…and your wife safe in your arms."

"Aye, Duncan," Niall said as he hugged Nora closer. "The O'Byrnes have much to thank you for this night…do we not, Ronan?"

"Aye, you have our thanks, FitzWilliam. Shall we ride with you to escort what's left of Sigurd's forces to Ostmentown?"

"No, I'll not have you risk danger by venturing too close to Dublin. Though I would have it otherwise, there is still a price on your heads. Donal MacMurrough and I will ensure that the bastards board their ships…and with their vow never to sail to Ireland again if they value their lives. The Ostmen will know as well never to march again into Leinster."

In the moonlight breaking through the stormy clouds, Nora could see that the faces of Niall, Ronan, and Duncan—Maire's Duncan!—were grim though tears glistened in Triona's eyes.

Grateful tears, Nora knew, as mayhap her courageous sister-in-law's prayers to see Maire again one day were that much closer to being answered.

No more was said, the men nodding to each other as Duncan FitzWilliam veered his mount away to rejoin his men in the camp below.

Until Triona broke the silence, calling out to him, "Give Maire our love!"

With a wave of his hand Duncan galloped down the hill, while Nora watched as Triona nudged her stallion Laeg between Niall and Ronan.

"Shall we get your bride home to Glenmalure, Niall O'Byrne? I believe we've postponed your wedding feast long enough."

Niall's arms tightened around Nora, while she looked up at the man who had so completely won her heart. "Aye, husband, take me home."

"Do you think they'll even attend their own wedding feast? They disappeared into their dwelling-house two days ago and we haven't seen them since!"

Triona laughed at Ronan's dark scowl, though she knew he wasn't angry at all.

Just hungry. Everything lay in readiness, the feasting-hall alight with torches and filled to the brim with their clansmen, wives, and children as all awaited Niall and Nora to join them.

The tables were laden with savory things to eat and cups were filled to the brim with wine or ale. The lanky wild-haired harper began another rousing tune to attempt to keep everyone distracted from the lengthening delay.

Even little Deirdre sitting on Triona's lap appeared impatient, and pounded her tiny fists upon the table. That made Ronan throw his head back and laugh, though he then shook his head at Triona.

"I fear she's even more willful than you, wife. Soon she'll be demanding a bow and arrows and a fine leather bow case just like her mother's, and a pony, and trousers—"

"Begorra, she's not even two, Ronan! Mayhap she'll prefer wearing pretty gowns like Nora and Maire, did you ever think of that?"

Ronan's snort told Triona that he knew as well as she Deirdre possessed a headstrong nature that one day would try them—ah, but those worries were for years ahead!

Mayhap, too, Deirdre would find herself with brothers to help keep an eye out for her and gentle-hearted sisters like Maire to temper her stubbornness. Triona had made no secret of her hopes to have a slew of children with Ronan. As if guessing her thoughts, he reached out to squeeze Triona's hand.

"Whatever the future brings, my beautiful bride of two years, we'll weather it together, aye?"

Triona nodded at Ronan, tears welling in her eyes although that wasn't like her at all. She knew it was the babe growing within her making her emotions so raw.

Because of their unborn babe, too, Ronan had urged her to remain at the stronghold rather than join him, Niall, their clansmen, and the MacMurroughs in going after Nora. Yet Triona had refused and saddled Laeg to ride with them, determined to do whatever she could to help them find her beloved sister-in-law.

Once he knew of Ronan's plan, Donal MacMurrough had decided to send half of his clansmen to Ferns to escort Caitlin home, and to alert his reinforcements to change their course to Glendalough. As the rest of them had headed north, they'd had no idea if Duncan FitzWilliam had answered Ronan's urgent message. Triona had wept then, too, when they had come upon Maire's husband and his armored knights on their way to Glenmalure!

Yet those grateful tears had been nothing to the ones she'd shed when they spied Nora running desperately from the camp with that vile Norseman so close upon her heels. Or when Triona had jumped from Laeg's back to rush to Nora's side and gather her terrified and blood-splattered sister-in-law in her arms to hug her close.

Or during the ride home when Nora had told them about her father and that Sigurd had thankfully not ravaged her—

"Sweeting, the danger is past and Nora is safe with us again," came Ronan's low voice to draw her from such thoughts, his thumb gently wiping a tear from her cheek.

It never ceased to amaze her that he could so easily read her mind, aye, and that he knew just when to soothe her by calling her 'sweeting' like her maid Aud used to do.

Triona so missed her, but Aud was living happily with her husband Taig O'Nolan, chieftain of the Blackstairs O'Nolans, in Carlow. It had been so long though, since Triona had seen Aud...and it felt so long since she had seen Maire.

Duncan probably wasn't home yet at Longford Castle so he could share with her that all was well and give her their love. Oh, how Triona wished there would be a day soon when they could all be together!

"Jesu, Mary, and Joseph, I must be a wretched sight," Triona said as she stood up and handed their wriggling daughter to Ronan. "I'll go and see what's taking Niall and

Nora so long."

"Not before a kiss," Ronan said huskily, his slate gray eyes darkened with emotion as she bent her head to oblige him.

His lips so warm against hers, Triona felt thrilled to her toes like she always did when kissing her handsome husband. Yet Deirdre's squeal of protest made both of them laugh, their beautiful wee daughter not liking at all that she had been smothered between them.

Nor was the mood in the feasting-hall growing any less impatient as Triona rushed to the doors, though the harper still played furiously to amuse everyone.

She was glad that Nora and Niall had enjoyed some time to themselves, and she'd made sure no one interrupted them other than maidservants with a plate of food, a pitcher of wine, or hot water for bathing. Yet if they didn't arrive soon, the evening's festivities might have to start without them!

Clansmen drinking and shouting out for more ale, their wives trying their best to control squirming children—dear God, where *were* they?

"Kiss me again."

Nora did, pressing her lips to Niall's for another breathless moment even though the tumult inside the feasting-hall seemed to grow louder. As his arms crushed her against him, she had never felt more loved...or more beautiful.

Niall had claimed as much when the maidservants stepped aside in their bedchamber so he might view their handiwork. Nora had twirled around for him in her lovely white and lavender gown chosen especially for this night while his admiring gaze had filled her with such joy.

Aye, the past two days had been filled with more contentment than Nora could have imagined as she and Niall had secreted themselves away in their dwelling-house simply to be alone and together.

To make love and free themselves from any misunderstanding, to laugh and savor the sweetness of being safe and sound in each other's arms.

Even now as Niall's kiss deepened, Nora felt such radiant happiness overwhelm her that she scarcely heard the huge doors to the feasting-hall thrown open. Triona's laughter made Nora gasp in surprise against Niall's lips.

"Well, Niall O'Byrne, will you be sharing your lovely bride with us this night or will you just stand there kissing each other?"

Niall's teasing smile thrilled Nora as the entire feasting-hall erupted in boisterous cheers and shouts of well wishes.

"What do you think, my love? I'd say we've worked up a fine appetite and it sounds like my clansmen are famished, too. Shall we join them?"

Nora nodded, smiling up at Niall as he clasped her hand and led her inside to their wedding feast.

*****

Read on for special bonus content, the heartwarming novella and Book 4 of The O'Byrne Brides Series, On A Wild Winter's Night!

On A Wild Winter's Night

MIRIAM MINGER

Publishing History

Digital edition published by Walker Publishing
Copyright © 2016 by Miriam Minger

Print edition published by Walker Publishing
Copyright © 2017 by Miriam Minger

ISBN: 978-1-943644-14-8

CHAPTER 1

Glenmalure
Wicklow Mountains, Leinster

"You gave me your word that you'd be civil, Ronan O'Byrne! Now stop scowling and at least try to look welcoming to Maire and her husband. Tomorrow is Christmas, after all, and they've ridden all the way from Longford Castle to share it with us!"

Triona felt relieved that Ronan's expression grew less forbidding as she turned her attention back to the stronghold's heavy gates being opened for their guests. She drew her fur-lined cloak more tightly around her in the crisp late afternoon air.

The day she had so fervently prayed for had finally come!

She could no longer contain her excitement and she rushed forward, though being so heavy with child made her gait more like the waddling of a goose. She could not believe how big she had grown and she still had several weeks to go before the birth of her and Ronan's second child!

"Easy now, sweeting! Will you alarm us all with your dashing about?" came Aud's no-nonsense chiding as her beloved former maid caught up with her and drew her to a stop. Aud might be a spare woman, but her strong grip brooked no argument. "You'll have your babe right here in the yard—begorra, now *that* would be a fine greeting for Maire and Lord FitzWilliam!"

Before Triona could answer, she felt the strength of Ronan's arm around her waist. She glanced up at him gratefully, glad that he'd come to her side, too.

In truth the preparations for their guests had exhausted her these past days, but she had wanted everything to be perfect for Maire and Duncan's visit.

Enough food for ten holiday feasts awaiting them. The O'Byrne men dressed in new tunics and trousers and the women resplendent in colorful gowns as befitted the special occasion. Aye, even the children and babes in arms had new clothes. Dozens of clanswomen had outdone themselves to make it so in three weeks' time!

Triona leaned against Ronan as the thundering of horses' hooves grew louder. Her huge gray wolfhound Conn had appeared as well and bounded over to join them, plopping down at Triona's feet.

Ronan had only agreed to extend the invitation a month ago, though Duncan had sent a message back to Glenmalure a week later that he and Maire would be pleased to join them for Christmas. Thank goodness Aud and her jovial husband, Taig O'Nolan, chieftain of the Blackstairs O'Nolans, had arrived from Carlow to help with the preparations and to stay until after the babe was born.

Niall and Nora had lent a hand as well, her kindhearted sister-in-law never far from Triona's side. Niall had focused upon doing his best to soothe Ronan's unease at having yielded to Triona's fervent wish that the entire family, Irish *and* Norman, be together at Christmastime.

Triona glanced over her shoulder to where Niall stood with his arm around Nora. The two of them made a loving and devoted pair if ever there was one, Niall so handsome and Nora with her thick auburn hair framing her face and looking radiant beside him.

And no wonder she was radiant! Nora's hand had drifted to her gently rounded stomach, aye, another O'Byrne babe, due to arrive in the spring. As Niall and Nora smiled with encouragement at her, Triona felt a strong kick inside her belly that made her gasp aloud.

"Triona?" Ronan's slate gray eyes were full of concern as he drew Triona closer.

"I'm all right, just our son making his presence known."

Ronan bent his head to tenderly kiss her cheek, both of them sharing the belief that this babe must be a boy for how vigorous his kicking and flailing. As the first riders in the entourage cleared the gates, Triona held Ronan's gaze. Tenderly she reached up to sweep midnight hair from his forehead.

"Thank you, husband. I know it's a hard thing for

you…but this day means everything to me."

He didn't have a chance to reply as suddenly the stronghold yard was filled with prancing horses, steam puffing from their nostrils. Triona counted four knights and eight men-at-arms, and in the midst of them Maire seated atop a snow-white mare and Duncan FitzWilliam astride his massive bay stallion. They, too, were all dressed resplendently as one would expect of the Baron of Longford and his entourage.

For a moment Triona felt her feet frozen to the ground, she was so struck by the sight of Normans within the O'Byrne stronghold.

Not enemies come to do battle, but there to celebrate Christmas among family.

Family!

"At least he didn't bring an army," Ronan muttered, his arm tightening around Triona.

Apprehension suddenly gripped her—Jesu, Mary, and Joseph, had she pushed him too far to agree to such a visit?—but she did her best to tamp it down.

No, she wouldn't allow anything to mar this occasion! Ronan would be fine for the three days Duncan had said they would stay, Niall had sworn he would see to it. After all, Duncan and his men had answered Ronan's call this last summer to help save Nora from Sigurd Skullcrusher! What stronger bond could have been forged between these two formidable men than that one?

"Welcome, FitzWilliam!"

Ronan's roar above the melee made Triona jump,

gratitude filling her that he hadn't remained stonily silent at her side. Conn jumped, too, and ran off to sniff at the horses.

As Aud rejoined her big bear of a husband standing near Niall and Nora, Triona felt Ronan clasp her hand and together they went to greet their guests. Already Duncan, as tall as Ronan and striking with his dark brown hair and eyes, had dismounted to lift his wife from her horse. Maire's teary smile made Triona's eyes well up, too.

"Oh, Triona! Ronan!" Throwing back the fur-trimmed hood of her cloak, Maire hastened toward them as best she could in spite of her limp, Duncan just behind her. Looking stunningly beautiful with her long black hair framing her angelic features, she flung her arms around both Ronan and Triona. "I'm so happy to be here! So happy!"

At that moment Triona felt all uneasiness disappear as Ronan crushed his younger sister in his embrace and lifted a laughing Maire into the air. He wasn't smiling when he released her so Triona could have a turn but he wasn't scowling, either.

In fact, she would swear she saw moisture in his eyes as she hugged Maire although he looked down briefly to brush it away. Her heart going out to him, Triona couldn't have been more proud of her fierce rebel husband when he turned to Duncan and locked forearms with him in greeting.

"You've my thanks again for riding to our aid last summer, FitzWilliam...and for taking such fine care of Maire. She looks well and healthy."

"She is life and breath to me and I wish for nothing more than her happiness," came Duncan's reply that warmed Triona's heart, too. "It would please me if you'd call me Duncan and I will call you Ronan. Agreed?"

As Ronan nodded, Triona relinquished Maire to Niall, who had come up behind them. Now tears did flow as the two embraced, Niall rocking his sister in his arms as she began to sob against his shoulder.

"Ah, Niall! When you disappeared last summer I didn't know if I would ever see you again! I was so worried about you, but you're here and whole—"

"Aye, and with a bride who's anxious to meet you. Shh, Maire, all is well. All is well…"

As Maire laughed with some embarrassment, wiping away her tears with the back of her hand, Triona had to blot her eyes, too. She could not have imagined a happier homecoming as Niall reached out his hand for Nora to draw her closer.

"Maire…this is Nora, my wife. You've two sisters now."

If Nora had felt shy at all to meet Maire, Triona would never have known it as the two young women hugged warmly.

Next Ronan introduced Duncan to Aud and Taig O'Nolan, Triona doubting the somewhat bemused-looking chieftain had ever met a Norman before in such convivial circumstances. And certainly not a Norman who was one of the most powerful barons in Leinster!

As everyone exchanged greetings and pleasantries amid

the low din of O'Byrne clansmen, their wives, and children watching the amazing scene, a strong cold gust of wind blew through the yard. The sun had already sunk below the surrounding mountains and snow flurries danced around them. Conn barked and jumped into the air trying to bite the swirling flakes. Triona saw then that Maire shivered and she drew her sister-in-law closer to her side.

"Ronan...Duncan, if you'll forgive our absence for a short while, I'd like to show Maire to her dwelling-house where she might revive herself from the long ride. We've so much to catch up on, too. Aud and Nora, will you accompany us?"

The two women smiled and fell in beside Triona and Maire as another brisk burst of wind swirled around them. Ronan's voice rose above the snorting horses and Conn's excited barking.

"Aye, we've places prepared for your men, FitzWill— Duncan, and my clansmen will tend to your horses. While we await our wives to rejoin us, let's adjourn to the feasting-hall where it's warm and the ale is waiting!"

"Oh, Triona, everything is just as I left it!" Maire looked around her with delight at the home she had last seen five months ago when Duncan had come to Glenmalure to claim her as his bride.

A home warmed by a glowing fire in the hearth and filled with beautiful things that Ronan and Niall had provided for her to brighten her days and lend her comfort:

Exquisite tapestries upon the walls, thick rugs underfoot, and a fine embroidered cloth upon the table. Candles glowed in every corner as if to welcome her. She'd led such a sheltered life here, happy enough, aye, and not ever imagining that things could ever be different for her...until Triona O'Toole had burst into their lives two years past and turned everything on its head.

It had been Triona who had softened Ronan's hard heart and forged a great love between them.

Triona who had helped Maire to grow stronger so she might walk without a crutch and enjoy horseback riding and fresh air and sunlight upon her face.

Triona who had introduced Niall to Caitlin MacMurrough only to have his heart broken...a terrible trial, to be sure, but one that had led him to finding his lovely bride Nora.

And now Triona who had convinced Ronan that they share Christmas together, Maire's eyes filling with tears that such a wondrous miracle had occurred.

"Maire?" Triona hastened to her side to squeeze her hand, and Nora and Aud drew closer, too, both women looking concerned.

"I'm happy, is all. To be here again...with all of you..." Her voice caught and she shook her head, composing herself. "I...I never thought it could happen."

"Aye, but it has and we're going to enjoy these three precious days that we have together," Triona said briskly as she drew Maire to a table where they all might sit down. "No tears, just smiles and laughter—and lots of it!"

They did laugh then, Triona taking her seat with great exaggeration as if her girth prevented her from sitting at all.

"This will be *you* soon enough, Nora O'Byrne!" Triona teased while Aud signaled for a maidservant to bring forth a tray of freshly baked bread sliced and slathered with butter. Another girl poured fragrant spiced cider into goblets.

Maire's hand strayed unconsciously to her own stomach, though she knew it would be weeks before she would show that she was with child. Her fondest dream had always been to become a mother. She had only just realized the much prayed for blessing a couple days ago—

"Maire...do you have something to tell us?"

She blushed to her roots, knowing at once that Triona had guessed her secret. She nodded, smiling, and before she could utter a word Triona had reached over to give her a heartfelt hug.

"Oh, Maire, this is such wonderful news!"

"Aye, but you mustn't breathe a word of it! Duncan doesn't know yet. I feared he wouldn't want me to make the journey—though I plan to tell him tomorrow on Christmas. It's my gift to him..."

As Nora came next to hug her and then Aud, all of them assuring her that they wouldn't spoil her surprise, Maire felt as if her heart might burst from their warm good wishes.

"Ah, my little Deirdre is awake from her nap and come to join us!" Triona held out her arms to her daughter who was deposited into her lap by a beaming maidservant.

Everyone cherished the beautiful child with her midnight curls and headstrong nature, her impish smile alone charming all who saw her. At once Deirdre wriggled out of her mother's embrace and made straight for Maire, the toddler opening her arms and giggling.

"I think she remembers me!" Thrilled, Maire swept up Deirdre and hugged her while laughter filled the room.

Truly, this Christmas among her family would be the most joyous of all!

CHAPTER 2

"The Justiciar John de Gray wants peace in Leinster, Ronan…and he speaks for King John. I, too, want peace in Leinster! He authorized me to tell you that he'll forgive the price on your heads if you swear to forever cease your raids against us."

As Duncan FitzWilliam's emphatic words resounded from the rafters, Niall felt a terrible sinking feeling and glanced around the holly bedecked feasting-hall.

All commotion had ceased. No one spoke. No one moved. All waited to hear what Ronan might have to say. From his darkening countenance, Niall knew it wouldn't be what Duncan hoped to hear.

Mounting tension thick in the air, Niall saw, too, that Duncan's knights and men-at-arms were suddenly stiff in their seats as if prepared for an imminent attack. Of words. Of swords. Who could say what Ronan intended to do? All Niall knew was that his efforts these past weeks to ease Ronan's mind about the reunion had suddenly, and mayhap irrevocably, been undone.

"So this is why you've come." Ronan's voice was low and furious, making the hairs stand up on the back of Niall's neck. He'd heard such a tone on occasion…and it was never good.

"I've come to please my beloved wife who longed to see her family again…and to carry the Justiciar's message," Duncan responded, his posture tense, too, but his voice steady and resolute. "As soon as I received your invitation, I sent word to John de Gray before I even spoke of it to Maire so I might know his mind about our making such a visit. You and your clansmen are rebels, Ronan. Wanted men for countless crimes against the Crown. Our presence here would not have been possible if the Justiciar hadn't agreed to it."

"And you riding to Glendalough five months ago when Donal MacMurrough and I requested your aid? Was that sanctioned as well by your all-powerful Justiciar John de Gray?"

Duncan didn't readily answer as if weighing his words, while Niall saw that Ronan's expression had grown only blacker. That made Niall take a draft of ale, while everyone in the feasting-hall remained ominously silent. God help them, this exchange wasn't going well at all!

"Your message was urgent, Ronan. There wasn't time to involve the Justiciar. You know that Donal MacMurrough is a trusted ally of King John. I could do nothing else but answer your call. Sigurd Skullcrusher's Norsemen, and the Ostmen that joined them on their march, threatened the peace—"

"There is no peace and well you know it, FitzWilliam!" Ronan slammed his fist down upon the table and lunged to his feet. "Not as long as you accursed Normans live and breathe in Éire! As chieftain of the Glenmalure O'Byrnes, I would no more agree to your Justiciar's offer than thrust a sword into my own heart! We will *never* bow to Norman tyranny!"

"Ronan…" Niall had risen, too, but he said nothing more at the dark scowl that Ronan threw at him. Then his brother fixed his furious gaze once more upon Duncan.

"If not for the love that my wife bears for her family— *all* of her family—I would have you and your men escorted from the stronghold this very moment! But instead *I* will leave and only return in three days when the lot of you are gone!"

A furor erupted as Ronan left Duncan staring after him to stride grim-faced through the throng of O'Byrne clansmen who rose as if to join him. Niall made to follow him, too, yet Ronan gestured for everyone to retake their places. Clearly, he meant to go alone and for the rest of them to make the best of what remained of this ill-fated visit.

Then Ronan was gone, the great doors to the feasting-hall closing shut behind him.

Niall was tempted again to go after him, but his instincts told him the thing was done. He knew Ronan well enough to know that nothing would sway him.

In truth, too, he did not dare leave Duncan and his men surrounded and outnumbered by O'Byrnes that looked ready to pitch a battle at any moment.

Instead Niall sighed heavily and retook his seat as Ronan had indicated. As his brother's Tanist, his clansmen followed his lead, albeit reluctantly.

"Well, Triona's not going to be pleased about this turn of events," he said almost to himself, although from Duncan's low curse he guessed that his Norman brother-in-law had heard him and was thinking about Maire's reaction, too.

Damn it all, had there ever been such a thing as a peaceable family reunion?

"Begorra, ladies, I fear we've lingered here too long. Ronan will surely be wondering what's become of us," Triona said as she rose heavily to her feet. At once Aud was at her side to help her, which made Triona erupt into laughter at herself. "Oh, Aud, have you ever seen such a sight? I'm big as a cow and with two weeks or so to go by my reckoning!"

"Mayhap not, sweeting." Aud clucked her tongue and shook her dark head. "By *my* reckoning, I'd say you've a day or two left before you'll have a newborn babe at your breast."

"Would you like Maire and me to go ahead and tell them you're on your way?" Nora asked, carrying Deirdre. Triona smiled as she shook her head and reached out to caress her daughter's cheek.

"No, let's all go together…the three O'Byrne brides!"

Then she laughed again. "Aye, and an O'Nolan bride with us, too, my beloved Aud, and one day my sweet Deirdre!"

As they all donned their cloaks and moved to the door, Maire fell behind and Triona glanced back at her.

"Maire?" Triona saw that her sister-in-law's lovely gray eyes were misty again with tears, but she knew they were happy ones as Maire gazed around the candlelit room and then caught up with them.

The door swung open, and Triona wasn't surprised to see that a foot of snow covered the ground and spilled across the threshold...with more coming down. The wind had grown fiercer and the air colder, and she at once covered her head with her warm hood. So did the others, Nora holding Deirdre close and making sure she was well bundled up.

As they moved together in a huddle into the torchlit yard, Triona *was* surprised, though, that the inner gates to the stronghold were wide open and a group of clansmen clustered there.

At once she felt a niggling of alarm, although she told herself to remain calm. Yet it was a strange thing for the gates to be open when everyone had gone to the feasting-hall...

She saw it then, fresh tracks in the snow leading from the stable to the gates.

A single rider from the looks of it, riding hard and fast. Jesu, Mary, and Joseph, whatever could have happened to make someone gallop out into the night?

Triona began to trudge faster through the snow toward

the feasting-hall, her heart suddenly pounding in her chest. She felt a sharp pain across her belly, but bit it back.

The same plaguing question taunted her. *Whatever could have happened to make someone gallop out into the night?*

Intuition gripped her. She was scarcely aware that she'd turned away from the feasting-hall to make her way instead to the gates until Aud, Maire, and Nora came hurrying after her.

"Triona, where are you going?" Aud cried out, but Triona ignored her former maid, her pulse racing now.

Her heart thundering.

Something telling her that events had suddenly gone terribly, terribly wrong though she yet had no basis for it.

She didn't see Nora turn back with Deirdre to hurry through the snow toward the feasting-hall. Triona didn't stop until she'd reached the massive gates, struggling to catch her breath as the clansmen there had begun to close them.

"No, wait!" Triona shook off Aud's hand upon her arm, and ignored Maire pleading for her to accompany them to the feasting-hall where it was warm. As the clansmen ceased their task to face her, Triona saw from their grim expressions that her intuition was not unfounded. "Why are the gates open? Who rode out?"

Only one man seemed to have the heart to step forward even as he glanced uncomfortably at the others. "Your husband, my lady."

Oh no, oh no, oh no! For a moment Triona felt her knees grow so weak that she feared she might crumple into the snow. Yet in the next instant she rushed past the men through the inner gates, though the second set built into a massive earthen rampart was already closed and barred. Just as the outer gates were already barred, giving her no way to run after Ronan.

For that was exactly what she was doing, desperation seizing her. Wildly she looked around her and saw the wooden steps leading up to the parapet atop the middle rampart.

Distantly she heard Aud screaming for her to stop. Maire crying out for her to stop.

She didn't heed them, instead clambering up the steps even as another pain seared across her belly stronger than the last. Yet still she climbed, not stopping until she had hauled herself onto the parapet where she stared out into the dark and now blinding snowfall.

"Ronan!"

Hot tears coursing down her frozen cheeks, she cried out his name again and again but the howling wind seemed to suck away the sound. Her hood had fallen, a strong gust whipping at her hair. Frantically she ran along the rampart, stumbling and scraping her hands upon the rough timber as she caught herself.

"*Ronan!*"

Her voice now raw, hoarse, Triona had begun to sob so inconsolably that she didn't hear a familiar voice behind her, shouting her name. Instead, she collapsed as a pain so fierce gripped her that she screamed in sudden agony, a warm wetness running down her legs.

"Triona!"

She barely recognized Niall who'd come up behind her, her eyes were so clouded by tears. She felt herself lifted into strong arms. As if from a faraway place she heard him breathing hard as he ran with her along the rampart and then carried her down the steps.

She heard more shouts and her wolfhound Conn's frantic barking. Unknown hands reached up to take her from Niall and then another pair of strong arms held her fast as she felt the man's powerful strides.

"Oh, Duncan, I think she's having the baby!"

Maire's voice, frantic, terrified…and then Niall's voice again as a door was kicked open and commands to stoke the fire in the hearth and to fetch hot water filled the air.

"Ah, sweeting…my poor sweeting."

Vaguely Triona felt Aud's familiar touch upon her brow until blackness overwhelmed her, Ronan's name upon her lips.

"No, Duncan, we cannot leave now! Triona needs me…needs all of us!"

Duncan sighed heavily at the tears brimming in Maire's eyes, her gaze so desperate, pleading.

His gut instincts were clamoring to leave the stronghold no matter that Triona moaned in childbirth in the adjacent bedchamber.

No matter that the winter storm had dumped another foot of snow since she had been carried to her and Ronan's dwelling-house several hours ago amidst frantic alarm and chaos.

Thankfully the wind had ceased to howl and a bright full moon had broken through the clouds, so they would have light to guide their way.

The worst of the snowfall was past and even now, his men awaited his command that they mount up and ride out of Glenmalure. The journey home to Longford Castle in Meath would not be an easy one, but they had ridden through worse.

Yet Maire had never traveled in such conditions, which had been the important consideration that had prevented him from ordering that they ride out hours ago in spite of the storm.

That, and Niall O'Byrne asking him to stay at least until after Christmas day for Triona's and Maire's sake. A far more reasonable man than his hotheaded brother, Niall had swayed him until Duncan saw the snowstorm had abated when he'd gone to check on his men. He'd returned at once to talk to Maire. If they were going to leave tonight, now was their opportunity...

"Maire, we're no longer welcome here. I told you what occurred between myself and your brother—"

"Aye, because you asked Ronan an impossible thing! If I'd known you carried such a message from John de Gray, I would never have come here! How could you, Duncan? You knew how much seeing my family again meant to me!"

As tears tumbled down his wife's lovely face, Duncan had to swallow hard at his sharp sense of remorse. He could have waited to share the Justiciar's proposal with Ronan until the end of their stay—but God's teeth, he had a duty first and foremost to the Crown! The vast barony he'd been granted in Leinster by King John depended upon his unswerving allegiance!

"The storm is past, Maire. I hope one day you will forgive me, but we must go—"

"God help us, Niall! Where's Niall?"

At Aud's desperate cry as she burst from the bedchamber, her husband Taig O'Nolan lunged from his chair by the hearth.

"He's ridden out after Ronan. Said he knew where to find him. What is amiss, wife?"

"Oh, Taig, I fear for Triona! The pains grow worse but she's losing her strength. With Nora and Maire's help, I've done what I can for her but she needs her husband. I came out to tell Niall that he *must* find him. Ah, God, may he bring Ronan home in time!"

His ruddy face gone pale, the stout chieftain glanced to where Duncan and Maire stood near the door to the dwelling-house.

"It wasn't my thought to overhear you and your lady, Lord FitzWilliam, but Niall left me in charge while he's gone. If you wish it, I'll have the gates opened for you straightaway."

From Maire's stricken look, once again her eyes pleading with him, Duncan knew that they would be riding nowhere this night. He nodded toward the bedchamber. "Go. Be with Triona."

"Oh, Duncan!" Maire flung her arms around his neck to hug him fiercely, and he pulled her against him to hug her back.

Yet only for a moment before he released her and she hastened as best she could away from him to disappear into the bedchamber with Aud.

CHAPTER 3

Ronan stared into the flickering flames, the peat fire he'd built in the hearth finally warming the stone hut he and Niall sometimes used when hunting.

The shrieking wind had subsided but up here in the forested hills beyond Glenmalure, the snow was piled thick and deep.

He had no food and no water other than to melt some of that snow, but damn it all, what did he care? At least he was no longer among enemies who yearned to make the O'Byrnes their vassals like so many other Irish clans who had ceased to resist the invading Normans.

By God, *he* would not yield as long as he held breath and life to fight them! To raid against them if any dared to step foot upon O'Byrne lands and attempt to settle there. He prayed Duncan FitzWilliam and his men had already left the stronghold to carry his response forthwith to Dublin Castle, and that the Justiciar John de Gray would choke upon it!

Ronan swore under his breath and drew his heavy

cloak more tightly around him, the copper-colored flames reminding him of Triona's fiery hair.

Aye, her fiery temper, too, which no doubt she would unleash upon him as soon as he returned to the stronghold. That, and her tears...for if Duncan was gone, then Maire would be gone, too, and never to return.

Ronan felt a sharp pang at that thought, but he quickly hardened his heart against it and scowled into the fire.

This disastrous reunion had been folly from the start, but he had surrendered to Triona's appeals for such an event because he knew how much it would please her. These last few months of her pregnancy had taxed her greatly...so much more than anything she'd suffered with Deirdre. It seemed her tears were always at the ready, unlike anything he'd seen from her before, and he couldn't bear to see her cry.

Ronan shifted uncomfortably upon the bench, imagining how she must have taken the news of his sudden departure—damn it, no, he didn't want to think about it!

Instead he glanced at the straw-filled pallet in the corner where he might as well attempt to get some sleep. Or he could step outside now that the snowstorm had subsided and check upon his horse sheltered beneath a lean-to built against the hut. At least there was a bag of oats left from a previous visit to feed the beast.

As for himself, he would have to go hunting in the morning if he wanted to eat, which made him think of the magnificent feast Triona had arranged for Christmas day. Roasted meats—venison, beef, and wild boar—and savory pies of mince and currants and crusty loaves of bread, all to be washed down with ale and honey mead.

Aye, it must be near midnight now, a holy night. A night of peace that he might have spent with Triona and among his clansmen if he had not agreed against his better judgment to share it with hated Normans!

"Enough!" Ronan shouted to the four walls. As furious as when he'd ridden away from the stronghold, he rose from the bench even as he heard his stallion neighing and snorting…and then someone shouting his name.

"Ronan, are you here? By God, answer me!"

Niall! What the devil…? Ronan threw open the door in a swirl of snow and rushed outside to see his brother dismount and lunge through drifts up to his thighs to reach him.

"Ronan, it's Triona! The babe is coming but she was so distraught after you left! I heard her through the door to your bedchamber crying out your name and I knew I had to find you. I fear for her life, brother!"

Ronan felt the blood drain from his face, Niall's expression so stricken that an icy chill gripped his heart.

Triona.

Cursing himself for ever leaving her and cursing even more the distance that separated them, Ronan ran for his horse.

God help him, if anything happened to his beloved wife or his unborn child, he would never forgive himself. Never!

***

"Hold her hand, Duncan! Tightly!" Aud commanded as Triona screamed in agony and bore down. "It doesn't matter that you're not Ronan. Your strength will give her strength—aye, I see the top of the child's head!"

Jesu help her! Nora stood beside Aud, ready to assist if asked and feeling flushed from the warmth of the room. She had never seen childbirth before, but she didn't feel afraid. Only terribly concerned for Triona who was in such pain, though Duncan's presence had steadied her and made her so much more alert.

Aud had drawn him into the bedchamber only moments ago with an urgent cry—"We need you, Lord FitzWilliam! Ronan isn't here so you must help us!"—and from then on, events had taken a miraculous turn.

It was as if Triona believed she was holding Ronan's hand, which she gripped so fiercely that her knuckles were white. As white as the linen sleeping gown she wore that was now damp with sweat, her knees raised and shaking.

Maire stood next to her husband holding his other hand and looking quite pale, no matter she'd attended Deirdre's birth and wasn't as new to witnessing childbirth as Nora. Yet both of them were determined to remain with Triona, and murmured words of encouragement as Aud leaned closer to the edge of the bed.

"Aye, Triona, push! Push!"

Her eyes closed, her face bright red as she held her breath and grimaced with effort, Triona did as Aud bade her until suddenly, Aud gave a cry of elation.

"A son, Triona! You and Ronan have a fine son!"

Nora started at the sharp slap that Aud gave the babe's bottom, and then the most outraged, lustiest outcry filled the room.

At once Triona collapsed backward upon the bed though she still gripped Duncan's hand, everyone smiling their relief and grateful tears welling in Nora's eyes. Maire too, had tears tracing her cheeks. She glanced up at Duncan with an expression of such love that Nora felt a pang in her heart.

When would Niall return home? Had he found Ronan? She hadn't known that Niall had left the stronghold to ride out into the snowstorm until Aud had rushed into the adjoining room to beseech him to do just that.

Nora had felt such concern at the news…but intense pride, too, for her courageous and good-hearted husband.

How she loved him! How she longed especially now for his safe return with Ronan when such happy tidings awaited them!

Her eyes blurred with fresh tears, Nora watched as Aud expertly tied off and then dispatched with the cord, cleaned off the wriggling babe, and swaddled him in a warm blanket. She was just about to hand him to Triona, too, who smiled now through her own tears and reached out for her child when her face contorted with fresh pain.

"Sweeting?" Aud's sharp intake of breath sent a chill plummeting through Nora as she found herself with Triona's newborn son suddenly thrust into her arms.

"Triona, sit up again!" Aud commanded. "You must sit up and grab your knees. You've another babe on its way! I see a foot!"

At once anxiety filled the air as Triona, clearly exhausted from the first birth, struggled to oblige her. Duncan knelt with one knee upon the bed and threw his arm around her to assist her while Maire stepped away, looking truly frightened.

Triona bore down as best she could, but Aud's worried frown made Nora send a desperate prayer heavenward. Even the babe in her arms with his downy midnight hair began to wail as if fearing for his unborn twin.

As the moments passed and still no birth though Triona pushed mightily, Duncan once more gripping her hand, Nora's apprehension only grew.

Something was wrong! She felt it...they all felt it. Triona glanced with terror in her eyes from Duncan to Maire and then to her beloved former maid.

"Aud...?"

"Sweeting, you must push this one last time! Will you do that for me? Now take a big deep breath...and push!"

Triona's intense straining truly alarming to behold, Nora held her own breath as Aud caught the babe in her hands with a cry of relief.

"It's a wee girl, Triona! You and Ronan have another daughter!"

Yet no sooner had Aud uttered the words than her face went white. Her brow beaded with sweat as she worked over the child to clear out her nose and mouth, rub her motionless body, and then gently slap her bottom.

"Aud, why isn't she crying?" Triona demanded hoarsely. "Aud? I don't hear her. Aud!"

This time a sharp slap resounded in the room...and then another, but nothing. As Maire backed away even further from the bed and began to weep, Duncan left Triona's side and went to Aud. Grim-faced, he gestured for her to hand him the babe.

"Let me try...please."

Nora cradled Triona's whimpering son against her and stepped back, too. She had never felt such helplessness as Duncan took the limp silent babe from Aud and covered her tiny mouth and nose with his mouth...and blew a great deep breath into her.

And then another forceful breath and another...while Aud embraced Triona who had begun to sob inconsolably.

So inconsolably that they didn't hear the slightest intake of breath from the babe, though Nora saw her little arms begin to quiver.

Yet Duncan had heard it and he breathed into the babe even harder as her skin went from blue-tinged to pink right before their eyes.

This time they all heard a gasp from the babe and her outstretched limbs began to flail...and then the sweetest sound they could have ever imagined as she let out a long, piercing wail.

"Ah, God, thank you!" Triona cried out as Duncan placed the wriggling babe into her arms and went at once to embrace Maire, who collapsed against him.

"Duncan, you saved her!"

He didn't answer her, fearing for his own unborn child at Maire's ashen pallor. He swept her up and held her close against him as he carried her from the overwarm room, while Triona called out more tearful thanks after them.

Duncan had noticed his wife's hand stray to her stomach enough times during their journey to Glenmalure to guess she was with child. He almost turned back to Longford Castle when he'd first seen it, but he knew how much this reunion with her family meant to her. As he strode with her toward the door of the dwelling-house, he met Taig O'Nolan's concerned gaze from where the burly chieftain stood by the hearth.

"All is well, Taig. Triona gave birth to two healthy babes this night."

"*Two?*"

At Duncan's nod, the chieftain gave an astonished whistle but then he called after them, "What of Maire, Duncan? Is she ailing?"

"She needs some fresh air, is all. A good Christmas to you."

"Aye, a good Christmas to you and your wife as well!"

As Duncan stepped outside into the crisp night air, the snow crunching beneath his boots, Maire looked up at him. He'd failed to grab their cloaks, but they weren't going far. Relief surged through him that her color in the torchlight illuminating the stronghold already looked better.

"Oh, Duncan, it is Christmas already, isn't it?"

He hugged her closer and kissed her brow, but sudden

shouts and commotion erupting from the O'Byrne clansmen guarding the gates made him stride faster across the yard.

Clearly they must have spied Ronan and Niall returning home, which made Duncan glad for Triona and Nora. Yet the last thing he wanted was to come face-to-face with an irate Ronan Black O'Byrne after their regrettable exchange in the feasting-hall.

That Maire made no comment about the mounting uproar told Duncan how bone-weary she must be. For now she needed rest, but at first light they would set out for Meath. Once she was safe and sound at Longford Castle, he would then ride to Dublin with Ronan's message for the Justiciar John de Gray.

In truth, Duncan hadn't expected any other response from Ronan and he didn't blame him.

His Scots family on his mother's side had suffered bitterly from Norman oppression for years. Being half Scots, Duncan, too, had been foully mistreated by his three Norman half-brothers when their father died and his poor mother locked away in a tower until the day she died.

A bastard son and a madwoman claiming to be a properly wedded wife, that's how his Norman family had deemed them, no matter that his parents' marriage had been performed by a priest. The cruel memories to this day made gall rise in his throat, though he swallowed it down as he came to the dwelling-house where he and Maire were staying.

No, indeed, he didn't blame Ronan.

Duncan knew deep in his heart that if he was in his rebel brother-in-law's place, he would have given the same defiant answer.

CHAPTER 4

Ronan dismounted at a run, his fury reigniting as he spied Duncan across the yard carrying Maire toward their dwelling-house.

Aye, he loved his sister, but he wanted every last Norman gone from Glenmalure! He shoved open the door to his home with Niall hard upon his heels, his outrage that Duncan and his men lingered at the stronghold turning again to raw apprehension.

The dwelling-house was too quiet, too still. Ronan quickly removed his heavy cloak and threw it upon a bench, and Niall followed suit.

Light shone from the bedchamber at the opposite end of the main room and Ronan heard hushed voices. His heart thundering in his chest, he drew closer to the door.

God help him, if he had arrived too late…

"Ronan!"

Taig O'Nolan's welcoming bellow was like icy water splashing upon his face as Ronan entered the bedchamber to a sight he would never have imagined.

Beaming at him, the burly chieftain cradled a swaddled infant in his arms. Triona lay covered in blankets upon the bed and held a second babe in her arms.

"You're the father of twins!" Taig enthused though Aud, standing at the side of the bed near Triona, immediately shushed him.

"Will you frighten the wee things with all your hollering? Keep your voice down, husband, and hand Ronan his son!"

"Son?" Ronan stared from the wriggling infant placed in his arms to where Triona smiled weakly at him. He'd never seen her look so pale before, no, not even after Deirdre's birth. At once he went to her side, glancing from her to the sleeping babe with a wisp of red hair nestled against her.

"A girl, Ronan," Triona said with tears welling in her eyes. "Our little Deirdre has a brother now and a sister."

Ronan's eyes clouded, too, his remorse for leaving her to bear their children without him cutting him to the quick.

Swallowing hard, he had no voice to speak. It was only when Triona reached out her hand to him and he clasped it, feeling her warmth—God in heaven, that she was alive and well!—that he felt able again to breathe.

"Triona…forgive me…"

Without speaking she squeezed his hand. She gazed with such love at him that Ronan knew with intense gratitude and relief that she held no ill will toward him.

He couldn't say as much for his infant son, though, who suddenly flailed a chubby arm and cuffed Ronan on the chin with his fist. Niall's laughter behind him where he stood with his arm around Nora resounded in the room.

"Aye, Ronan, you've met your match in that one! Already squaring off with his father! What will you and Triona name him?"

Ronan met Triona's gaze and she softly said, "Conor. For my brother...and Ronan's dearest friend. We already agreed to it."

As everyone in the room nodded their approval, Nora asked gently, "And your daughter?"

Ronan shrugged, momentarily at a loss.

He and Triona had believed all along that they would have a son and hadn't considered any girl's names, which now clearly had been an oversight. He thought of his mother, Aileen, but when Triona squeezed his hand again, he sensed she had a name in mind.

"Eva. My birth mother's name...but also because it means 'life'." Triona looked down at the swaddled infant in her arms. "This little one is our Christmas miracle. If not for Duncan here with us, we might have lost her—"

"Duncan?" His voice low, terse, Ronan had immediately bristled. "He was with you during the birth?"

"I called him in, Ronan," Aud interjected from the other side of the bed. "If not for Lord FitzWilliam, you might have lost your wife this night as well as Eva and Conor. You weren't here, though I don't fault you for it— but my sweeting's strength was nearly gone. He held onto Triona's hand as I bade him—"

"Held your hand?" Meeting Triona's eyes, Ronan felt

anger overwhelm him. Irrational, aye, he knew it, but the thought that a Norman stood here in his stead was almost more than he could bear. "Triona?"

"Aye, so he did, and I'll never forget how he helped me…and helped our children. He saved our daughter's life, Ronan! Conor came first and then Eva, but she wouldn't start breathing no matter what Aud did to revive her. It was so terrible and I feared—we *all* feared she was lost! And then Duncan took her and blew into her mouth…and she's alive now for it!"

Tears streaking her cheeks, Triona held the child up to Ronan. "Go on! Hold her! And when you do I pray that you find it in your heart to thank the man that saved her instead of any longer thinking ill of him! Shame on you, Ronan O'Byrne!"

Sobbing now as Ronan took the child from her, Triona fell back against the bed and turned her face away from him. No sound came from anyone else in the room, everyone standing stock-still and staring at him.

Staring at him as he looked down at the two precious babes…Conor sucking on his tiny fist while Eva gazed up at him with soft gray eyes tinged with the same emerald green as her mother's.

Ronan didn't speak and scarcely breathed, his heart welling up with emotion that left him shaken.

Aye, he'd been a fool…a raging fool.

Holding his children close, one cradled in each arm, he glanced up to find Triona watching him, the softest, most tender smile upon her lips. Such love shone in her eyes that he knew she'd forgiven him…again.

Granting him not one or two…but a host of Christmas miracles this night.

"So you guessed during the journey that I was with child?"

Duncan pressed a kiss to Maire's lips, her breath a soothing balm to his troubled thoughts.

How he loved this woman! He drew back from her and nodded, which made her sigh softly.

"I wanted to surprise you…to tell you on Christmas as my gift to you. Now here it is Christmas and I have no other gift—"

"You've given me everything I could ever want, woman. Your heart. Your love. And now a babe on the way. I need nothing more." Duncan tucked the blanket more securely around her shoulders. "Go to sleep. Dawn will come soon enough and we've a long ride ahead of us."

Maire sighed again, but if she felt any disappointment that they were going to leave the O'Byrne stronghold first thing in the morning, she didn't voice it.

Instead she gazed into his eyes and said softly, "Thank you, Duncan. You've given me the most precious gift, too, seeing my family again. I know it wasn't the easiest thing for you…but you've made me very happy."

Emotion closed Duncan's throat, and all he could do was nod and press another kiss to her lips.

He had always considered himself to be a hardened

warrior…but his sweet wife could fell him with a word, a glance. And now she had thanked him when they both knew—God's teeth, how he wished it were otherwise!—that it was unlikely they would ever return to Glenmalure or that Maire would ever see her family again.

He rose from sitting beside her on the bed and dimmed the oil lamp atop the table, feeling almost sick at that moment for the grief that would cost her.

To not see Triona again or Niall and Nora…or Deirdre and the twins born this night. Why did the world have to be such a harsh place of strife and division…when all Duncan wanted to do was bring light and happiness to Maire's eyes?

So his agitated thoughts assailed him again, Duncan quietly leaving the bedchamber so Maire could get some much needed rest. She still looked too pale, though who wouldn't be after witnessing the trauma of the twins' birth? Yet he knew that Maire would not have wanted to be anyplace else, so great was her love for Triona—

"Damn it all!" Duncan's vehement curse echoed in the outer room filled with its feminine trappings that bore witness to the gentle life Maire had led before he'd met her. He hoped she had fallen asleep already and hadn't heard his oath. Meanwhile, he was certain that he would not be sleeping at all tonight for the thoughts plaguing him—

"What the devil?" A sudden pounding at the door made Duncan glance instinctively at his sword belt.

"Duncan, it's Ronan!"

Ronan? Still fully dressed, Duncan made his way instead

straight to the door. The last thing he needed to do was greet his brother-in-law, however quick to anger, with a weapon in his hand. He pulled open the door...coming face-to-face with the last person he expected to visit this late at night. Suddenly wary, he kept his voice low so as not to wake Maire.

"Is anything amiss?"

Ronan shook his head and thrust two cloaks at him. "You left them at my home."

"So I did." Duncan took the garments, perplexed. Ronan stared at him as if something was on his mind and yet he looked uncomfortable, too. For an awkward moment, they simply looked at each other and then Ronan cleared his throat.

"I saw you carrying Maire earlier. Is she well?"

So that was it, Duncan thought, tossing the cloaks onto a carved bench beside the door. "Sleeping. It was a trying night."

Ronan nodded, adding, "Aye, I just came from Triona's bedside."

"Is she all right?"

"She is...thanks to you."

Now it was Duncan who cleared his throat, astonished to say the least. Something was truly different about Ronan's demeanor...as if the tension Duncan had sensed in him since their arrival at the stronghold had disappeared. He gestured into the room. "Do you want to come inside?"

"No, I like the cold air...and it's not my intent to stay long. I am forever indebted to you, Duncan. If not for you, my wife and twins might not have survived this night…aye, especially little Eva."

"Eva. A fine name."

"It means 'life' and you breathed it into her." His voice gone hoarse, Ronan glanced down for a moment and when he looked up, Duncan saw moisture in his eyes. "As I said, I can never repay you…nor can I agree to the Justiciar's offer."

Silence fell between them except for Duncan's heavy sigh. Ronan looked resolute now and he shook his head.

"It's an impossible thing for me, Duncan—"

"I know."

Duncan wasn't surprised that Ronan looked as startled as he'd felt moments ago. "Mayhap Maire never told you that I'm half Scots, Ronan. I've family on my mother's side who hate the Normans as much as you." Duncan gave a humorless laugh. "Probably more as they've been railing against them longer…since William the Conqueror."

"Yet you're half Norman, too. You fight for them—"

"Since I was sixteen and joined King John's army to make my way in the world. One must take a stand and choose a side…as well you know."

"Aye."

Again silence fell and a heaviness, too, as if the weight and responsibility of their opposing worlds had settled upon them.

Duncan thought of Maire sleeping in the other room…while Ronan glanced over his shoulder toward the dwelling-house that sheltered Triona and his newborn twins. But finally it was Duncan who reached out his hand toward Ronan.

"We're family now no matter rebel Irish or Norman. Let's swear here and now to peace between us for the sake of those we love…our wives and our children. Agreed?"

Ronan took his hand firmly and nodded. "Aye, to peace between us."

"You must also swear never to raid on my lands in Meath or I will be forced to fight against you. Nor will those who answer to me ever trespass upon O'Byrne lands as long as I live and breathe."

"Agreed. I swear it."

"Good. Then it is done." Duncan released Ronan's hand at the same moment he caught a flash of white out of the corner of his eye…Maire in her sleeping gown at the threshold to the bedchamber. Ronan saw her standing there, too, his expression immediately softening.

"Maire…a good Christmas to you."

"And to you, Ronan. Is all well? The babes? Triona?"

"Aye. Conor and Eva were suckling hungrily when I left them…and it's time I head back." Ronan looked again at Duncan. "Will you stay with us the three days, brother? I believe our wives would be most happy to hear it. I, too, would be pleased…and honored."

Duncan heard Maire's soft intake of breath behind him as he nodded. "Three days."

No more was said as Ronan flashed a rare smile and then left them to stride across the yard, a gangly wolfhound suddenly running up to trot beside him.

Shaking his head and smiling, too, Duncan closed the door against the cold night air.

Yet he had no sooner turned around when Maire threw her arms around his neck, standing on tiptoes to kiss him.

"Are you pleased, my love?"

Triona glanced at Ronan, who cradled Conor in the crook of one arm and Deirdre in the other while Triona held Eva close against her. What a contrast, the two sisters! Deirdre wouldn't stop squirming to get a better look at her new brother while Eva slept peacefully in Triona's arms no matter the boisterous din in the feasting-hall.

A din of music and laughter and the sounds of Norman and Irish alike enjoying their Christmas dinner. Triona smiled with tears brimming in her eyes as she nodded. "Aye, husband, more than pleased."

Ronan hadn't wanted her to leave her bed so soon after childbirth but Triona wouldn't have missed this occasion for anything. So she'd asked him to fetch Deirdre from the clanswoman who had taken care of her during the night while Triona dressed and next bundled up the twins, and then together as a family they had joined the festivities.

"A good Christmas!" Niall shouted above the noise from where he sat with his arm around a smiling Nora at the head table.

"Aye, a good Christmas!" enthused Taig O'Nolan, who raised his brimming cup of ale while Aud beamed beside him. "To Conor and Eva O'Byrne!"

"To Conor and Eva O'Byrne!" came the resounding toast as everyone in the feasting-hall raised their cups.

Triona did not miss that Ronan threw a look of gratitude at Duncan, who nodded and drew a teary-eyed Maire closer against him.

Tears of joy that Triona shared as she kissed Eva's downy head.

*****

ABOUT THE AUTHOR

Miriam Minger is the bestselling author of emotion-packed action adventure historical romances that sweep you from lusty medieval times to Regency England—and with some dangerously seductive 18th century tales in between. With two dozen books published in five languages, Miriam is also the author of contemporary romance, romantic suspense, inspirational romantic suspense, and children's books. She is the winner of several Romantic Times Reviewer's Choice Awards—including Best Medieval Historical Romance of the Year for The Pagan's Prize—and a two-time RITA© Award Finalist for The Brigand Bride and Captive Rose.

Miriam loves to create stories that make you feel the passion, live and breathe the adventure, laugh and cry, and that touch your heart.

For a complete listing of books as well as excerpts and news about upcoming releases, and to connect with Miriam, visit www.miriamminger.com.

Made in the USA
Middletown, DE
20 August 2018